THROUGH THE MOON GATE

Borgo Press Books by JACQUELINE LICHTENBERG

THE SIME~GEN SERIES from The Borgo Press

House of Zeor, by Jacqueline Lichtenberg (#1)
Unto Zeor, Forever, by Jacqueline Lichtenberg (#2)
First Channel, by Jean Lorrah and Jacqueline Lichtenberg (#3)
Mahogany Trinrose, by Jacqueline Lichtenberg (#4)
Channel's Destiny, by Jean Lorrah and Jacqueline Lichtenberg (#5)
RenSime, by Jacqueline Lichtenberg (#6)
Ambrov Keon, by Jean Lorrah (#7)
Zelerod's Doom, by Jacqueline Lichtenberg and Jean Lorrah (#8)
Personal Recognizance, by Jacqueline Lichtenberg (#9)
The Story Untold and Other Stories, by Jean Lorrah (#10)
To Kiss or to Kill, by Jean Lorrah (#11)
The Farris Channel, by Jacqueline Lichtenberg (#12)

Other Jacqueline Lichtenberg Borgo Press Books:

City of a Million Legends
Molt Brother
Science Is Magic Spelled Backwards and Other Stories (Jacqueline Lichtenberg Collected, Book One) (ed. by Jean Lorrah)
Through the Moon Gate and Other Tales of Vampirism (line Lichtenberg Collected, Book Two) (ed. by Jean Lorrah)

THROUGH THE MOON GATE

AND OTHER TALES OF VAMPIRISM: JACQUELINE LICHTENBERG COLLECTED, BOOK TWO

JACQUELINE

LICHTENBERG

Edited by Jean Lorrah

THE BORGO PRESS

MMXI

THROUGH THE MOON GATE

FIRST EDITION

Published by Wildside Press LLC

www.wildsidebooks.com

DEDICATION

For John Betancourt at Wildside Press

and

Robert Reginald at Borgo Press,

Who had the idea to collect my short stories

CONTENTS

ACKNOWLEDGMENTS

THESE STORIES WERE previously published as follows, and are reprinted (with minor editing, updating, and textual modifications) by permission of the author:

"Vampire's Fast" was first published in *Galaxy Magazine*, Jan./Feb. and Mar./Apr., 1994. Copyright © 1994 by IDHHB, Inc. Copyright © 2011 by Jacqueline Lichtenberg.

"Truth Death" was first published in *Galaxy Magazine*, Issue #3, 1995. Copyright © 1995 by IDHHB, Inc. Copyright © 2011 by Jacqueline Lichtenberg.

"Vampire's Friend" was first published in *Heaven and Hell*, edited by Winifred Halsey, Speculation Press, 2002. Copyright © 2002, 2011 by Jacqueline Lichtenberg.

"Through the Moon Gate" was first published in *Tales of the Witchworld #2*, edited by Andre Norton, Tor Books, 1988. Copyright © 1988 by Andre Norton. Copyright © 2011 by Jacqueline Lichtenberg.

"False Prophecy" was first published in *Tarot Tales*, edited by Rachel Pollack and Caitlin Matthews. Century Legend, 1989. Copyright © 1989, 2011 by Jacqueline Lichtenberg.

Other Acknowledgments

Again and always thanks go to Ronnie Bob Whitaker for meticulously retrieving the texts done pre-word processor and on old, elderly, decrepit versions of Microsoft Word.

I also must thank Sue Stewart, Executrix to the Andre Norton estate, for allowing the use of my story "Through the Moon Gate," which opened a floodgate of ideas to be explored. Before I wrote that story, I didn't think I could do a supernatural vampire—now I'm totally engaged in this creature's existence. So "Through The Moon Gate" is a key item I wanted to present here.

Jacqueline Lichtenberg

FOREWORD

AND THEREBY HANGS A TALE

This collection presents two kinds of vampire—one that's the original vampire on earth, first of his kind, or of his line, created by two deities clashing for possession of him; and one that is descended from aliens from outer space via interbreeding with humans (*i.e.*, a science fiction vampire).

Either one could be the origin of all the myths about vampires and vampiric creatures, neither is what the vampire fan would ordinarily expect.

First we have Dorian St. James, sometimes known as Dorian St. John, Malory Avnel, Arnaud Lemieux and of course a host of other names over the millennia.

He was created, as I note in the afterword to "Through the Moon Gate" here below, in response to a request from Andre Norton for a story for her Witch World Collections. How could I resist that? But at the time I was developing my science fiction vampire universe (yes, shamelessly mixing genres) and no way would a science fiction vampire fit into such a gorgeous fantasy universe as The Witch World.

Also, at the time, I expected whatever character I

contributed to the Witch World would stay in the Witch World. So I needed a new vampire whose origin was in magic, not science. (a distinction I don't ordinarily make).

So all of a sudden, out of nowhere, this bat form flew through the night and fell through a Gate into the Witch World. Well, it didn't happen by accident. There was this woman on the Witch World who was on a journey searching for a teacher for her powers, and at just the right moment, she stumbled into an ancient relic and activated it.

Now what's a fine peasant girl to do with a dripping wet vampire?

I wrote to Andre Norton and presented a quick sketch of the idea—a vampire falls into the Witch World. She called me and said no, absolutely not. Nothing Evil like that would make it through. Me? Write an Evil Vampire? No way.

So I explained he was a good-guy vampire—at that time a very rare breed in literature except for Chelsea Quinn Yarbro's St. Germain character—whom I greatly admire.

And Andre Norton said to send her the story, so I did. And it was accepted for *Tales of the Witch World #2*.

The moment I saw it in print, I just had to figure out what was so good about this good-guy fantasy vampire that he deserved to fall into the Witch World and have a better life—um, existence.

Soon enough someone else asked for a story, and up

popped Dorian explaining himself. I asked Andre if I could tell the story of Dorian before he fell into the Witch World, and she said that would be fine.

So as I was asked for short stories, I wrote about Dorian wherever I could fit in a fantasy vampire, and the result to date is in this collection.

But there's more to this tale. Some years later, I was asked by an audio-only producer for short stories that could be adapted to a dramatized audio format. Of what I submitted, he chose The Dorian St. James saga, and to date has recorded one of the four available stories.

That dramatization was broadcast on XM Satellite Radio. I'm expecting the others will follow along with more stories of the origin of Dorian, and his adventures learning how to walk the fine line between good and evil when the rules of existence compel him to kill at least a couple times a month.

Meanwhile, my science fiction vampires have two novels extant, though not about the same characters. *Dreamspy* is set out in the galaxy amidst a far flung interstellar ecological war, where magic and science are virtually indistinguishable. In *Dreamspy* we discover the keys to many mysteries left hidden between the words in *Those of My Blood*.

One mystery revealed in *Dreamspy* is how it can possibly be that aliens from outer space can interbreed with Earth humans. Another is how the interstellar drive of the space ship that crashed on Earth's Moon actually works.

Those of My Blood is set just about "now" and a

bit into the future when we could create a Moonbase installation to study an alien space ship that crashes on the moon. The novel is essentially a Vampire Romance, very heavy on the Intimate Adventure. On the strength of that Romance element (which actually comes onstage in Chapter 4 of *Those of My Blood*) and my Dushau Trilogy (*Dushau*, *Farfetch*, and *Outreach*) that won me a Romantic Times Award, I was invited into a 7 author group-blog with Cindy Holby, Rowena Cherry, Margaret L. Carter (the same writer of vampire fiction and non-fiction mentioned in *Vampire's Friend*), Susan Kearney, Linnea Sinclair, and Susan Sizemore on the topic of Alien Romance.

Titus Shiddehara, the lead male character in *Those of My Blood*, is a young vampire, but already he's had several torrid love affairs, an engagement and a marriage, too.

But he's another one of the good-guy vampire characters who have learned hard lessons about how to relate to humans. And my question, as always after writing one of these characters, is how did he learn to be so good?

In the two short stories presented in this volume, you will discover the beginnings of one of Titus's hardest lessons—why he must use a very delicate touch on human minds when gripping a mentality with his Influence.

I originally wrote "False Prophecy" in response to a request for a story that was based on a Tarot Card, and I chose The Hanged Man. The sequel, "True

Hospitality," is one of those stories that just wrote itself as a springboard for a novel that has not as yet been written. Both these short stories are set about twenty years before *Those of My Blood.*

As you will see in "False Prophecy" and "True Hospitality," when Titus Shiddehara falls for Gabby, he is being seduced by the Light side of The Force!

As always my stories are Intimate Adventure. In this volume you will find that the Dorian St. James saga is an Intimate Adventure with barely a mention of a romance or love affair. But Titus Shiddehara, part human and proud of it, has a tendency to fall in love with certain dynamic women who become the source of his motivation.

Free chapters of the novels are posted and more information about current projects can be found at

http://www.simegen.com/jl/

Or:

http://jacquelinelichtenberg.com

Jacqueline Lichtenberg
Phoenix, AZ
2011

VAMPIRE'S FAST

Ever since I wrote "Through The Moon Gate" for *Andre Norton's Tales of the Witch World #2*, I've wondered what Dorian St. James did to deserve falling through a gate into the Witch World. This tale explores his origins and nature long before that event. See the story, "Through the Moon Gate," below.

The charred lump of flesh in his arms had been his daughter, or the closest thing to a daughter that his kind could know.

The vampire who, in San Francisco, called himself Malory Avnel, or sometimes Dorian St. James, gently lay the remains on the soft velvet couch, reading the area with all his senses. There were faint impressions in the lush rose carpet, mortal footprints. A mélange of scents lingered in the apartment as did faint, indefinable and unnamable traces of psychic presence.

As he knelt beside the blackened corpse, the events unrolled in his mind as if he were remembering them, though he'd been nowhere near at the time.

Rita had been sleeping the day away, as their kind must. Two large men had broken in. He could almost see them. Well groomed. Cologne. Hair spray. Freshly dry-cleaned wool suits. Real leather shoes. Guns. Garlic. Newly sawn ash stakes. Perhaps even silver crosses.

If he ever encountered them, he'd know them by their body odor. Scrubbing and deodorant couldn't hide it. No two humans smelled alike. Most probably these two worked for Don Jose del Rio, the latest success in the drug import business.

It was Malory's habit to take the two kills a month he needed from among humans who killed other humans for profit. He considered drug dealers in that category since most modern addictions were deadly. Lately, he'd been preying on del Rio's middle-management, a singularly superstitious lot.

A few weeks ago, Malory had been surprised while feeding on a particularly satisfying kill, and had left the scene before disposing of the exsanguinated corpse.

Rita had also been feeding on del Rio's organization, and it was possible that she, too, had made an error, leading them to her. Or they might have found her through him.

The killers had left none of their paraphernalia behind. They hadn't needed to use it. Rita was so very young. Even when dragged from her sanctuary into the bright sun slanting in the window—it must have been about four p.m. from the angle—she hadn't been able to rouse herself enough to put up more than a token struggle.

Her sleeping robe was torn. There were broken bones

in her left foot. And Malory hadn't been there to help.

Shaking with emotions he couldn't name, he knelt, gently placing his hands on the charred skull. It crumbled. "Rita, I swear by the gods of my fathers, the next blood I feast on will be that of your murderer—however long it takes."

His chin dropped to his chest, and he choked on the unutterable need to cry. But of course, he could not. He yanked himself away from the remains and went to the well concealed closet which was her sanctuary. He'd had workmen build it into the back wall of her kitchen, concealed to look like a shallow pantry. Then, he had erased their memories.

Now the shelf unit stood out from the wall next to the door. Inside, the bed was rumpled, a gold satin sheet spilling out onto the floor with a dirty shoe mark on it.

The whistling tea kettle had been knocked off the stove and lay on its side in a puddle.

He could almost hear her screams.

He shuddered, fighting the inward visions, the pain.

A long time later, careful to leave no trace of himself, he gathered the sheets, sealed the closet and snapped the pantry shelves in front of it, breaking the lock so the next tenant would not find it. He cleaned up the tea kettle.

Then he rolled the charred remnants in the sheets, carried the bundle to the basement and disposed of it in the incinerator. It was the new, non-polluting kind. Even as young as she'd been, there'd be no traces left of a body.

And now, he knew, he needed help—mortal help. With the negligence of millennia of practice, he took bat form.

By three a.m. he was outside a town house a few blocks from his own house, high on a cliff overlooking the ocean beach—an area that was usually heavily fogged in. He still had a few hours until the sun would drive him to sanctuary.

Resolute, he turned to mist and sifted through the screen into the bedroom of David Silver.

The human was snoring. Malory watched him fondly for a few moments, then whispered, "Dave! Dave, wake up!"

The snoring arrested in mid-breath, and with a mumble and a start, David Silver sat up in bed. Then he relaxed. "Oh, it's just you. Wha'time'sit?"

Malory told him, and Silver swore. "Why do you do this to me? Don't you know I need to sleep at night?"

"Rita's been killed."

"Oh. Is she okay?"

"No! Mortals broke into her sanctuary and exposed her to the sun. She's gone. True Death."

"Oh, no!" This time it was a cry of grief. For a time, the two had been lovers. Then Rita had become involved with Malory and decided to accept immortality, leaving Silver with this house and a whopping mortgage. Malory had extended the same offer to Silver, but he'd refused emphatically.

Malory waited as Silver worked through the shock, the brief rage at Malory for making her a vampire, the reverse of blame to himself for letting her do it, and the realization that it had been her choice to make. And then there were wracking sobs that didn't pass quickly at all.

Malory sat on the bed and put an arm around Silver's shoulders. For the vampire, the human's tears were a necessary cleansing he needed to share. When it was over, he felt the release into calm acceptance that he could not have achieved on his own. He let his forehead rest on Silver's shoulder, against his neck, to enhance the contact.

Sniffing, Silver asked, "Are you hungry?"

Malory pulled away. "No. I fed well only last night. I have sworn the next blood I take will be her killer's."

Silver pushed his bedclothes aside and threw on a robe. "Come on," he said leading the way to the kitchen. "Tell me the whole story. I have to know it all."

As Silver drank black coffee, Malory recounted what he knew. "So, Dave, I'm sworn to get them—and their boss as well. But I'm going to need help. Mortal help."

Silver studied the dregs of his coffee. "I'm a tailor. I don't even have my own business. I work for a department store. I was never even in the army. I'm in terrible shape and I'm hopelessly clumsy. What can I do that you can't?"

"Stay awake in the daytime—as my foes do."

"Foes. How poetic."

"I'm sorry. I read a lot."

Silver gave him a cockeyed smile. "Foes. Okay.

They killed her. They're my foes, too. What do I do?"

"Guard me in the daytime. Let me use you to enlarge my sphere of awareness so none can come upon us unwarned."

"Malory, I can't guard you all day. I have to work."

"Quit your job. I'll put you on my payroll at double your current salary. Afterwards, you'll get a bonus that will let you open your own shop. Deal?"

"I didn't know you were that rich."

"I've had a while to work at it."

"I suppose. You've never said how old you are."

"I don't exactly know." He shrugged. "Millennia. Aren't you going to ask me what you really want to ask?"

"You keep saying you can't read my mind."

"It's more empathy and knowledge of human nature than telepathy. I said I want to use you, and you haven't objected to that. Why?"

"I hate thinking about what you are."

"If you're going to help me, you must think about it. You'll be my spare hands and eyes. I'll ruthlessly compel your actions—and they won't be slow or clumsy. If it comes to a fight, I'll use your body regardless of the injury it might take. But Dave—you could die."

Silver was looking at him as if he'd never seen him before. "You could do all that?"

"It's not even difficult."

"But you've never—I mean, I've never felt you...."

Malory reached across the table and took the man's

hands in his own. "I wouldn't ever without your permission. Oh, I do erase memories, for my own security. And I cast illusions about myself. And I take blood from unknowing donors who never miss it. And, Dave, you know I kill humans for my own needs. But I have my own code of honor. I give you my word I've never used you, and I won't without your permission."

Silver studied him warily. "I can't quite imagine what it would feel like, but the thought makes my skin crawl."

"I could make it so you felt nothing—or I could take the memory away and leave a hole in your time, or I could fill it with the illusion of a Hawaiian vacation."

Silver pulled away and went around the counter into the kitchen to get more coffee. He came back chewing on one nail and stared out the sliding door to the patio. "I don't want to lose the memory or remember something that didn't happen. I want to feel and remember whatever happens to me. For me, life is to be lived, every detail of it, right to the end. And it should end all in God's own good time."

"If you like, I'll show you what it's like to be used."

Back to the vampire, Silver whispered, "Okay. Do it."

Malory closed his eyes and mentally reached for Silver, infiltrated his mind and took over his body. He made him walk back to the table, turn three times in place without sloshing the coffee, sit down, sip his coffee, and set the mug down without even rippling the surface. Then he made him grin and say, "That's amazing!" Then Malory let go.

That was the mistake. At the sudden return to normal, Silver turned white, lips slightly green, and plunged into the kitchen where he stood gripping the sink and gasping as if expecting to heave up all the coffee he'd drunk.

Malory was beside him in a blink, knowing that if he suppressed the nausea, he'd turn the man against him forever. He'd had permission for one demonstration, not two. So he just held Silver close. "I'm sorry. It's my fault. Breathe deeply. Hang on and breathe. It'll pass in a moment."

And it did. Malory led him back to the table, explaining, "I let go too abruptly for you. Most people don't react so violently. It won't happen again."

"Mal, I don't think I can take that. Even before— everything came unstuck—it was awful. I wasn't me. I even heard myself speak in my own voice, and it wasn't me."

His tone was the first indication Malory had that Silver had made up his mind to accept. "I can make it so you won't feel a sense of being—invaded—out of control."

Silver shook his head. "I don't want—. Malory, if I don't help you, what are you going to do?"

"I'm sworn. I will kill them—one way or another."

"That's another thing. I don't want to kill anyone. I just want to put them in jail."

"For murdering a dead woman? Whose remains don't exist?"

"Yeah." But he added, "Do you know how many times they jail the wrong person for murder, no matter how careful they are? How can we be sure we've got the right people?"

"I can identify the hit men. I only have to find them and discover who they work for. Then I've a plan, but I won't tell you unless you're with me—or I'd have to erase your memory to be sure it couldn't be tortured out of you."

His gaze went to the graying light behind the windows. "Oh, Lord, they could be out there. They could have followed you. They could be coming after us right now."

"They didn't. They aren't." At Silver's look, he said, "Being a vampire has to be good for something. Still, you're right, they just might trace you through Rita, and me through you. In the past, I've been attacked in my sanctuary during the day. The prospect frightens me, so I'm asking you to let me use you."

"And you had to find her like that. It must have been hell on you." He scrubbed his face. "You mean, using me, you could be aware of things that are going on even in the daytime, when you're asleep?"

"Yes. I need that because these people know the weaknesses of my kind."

"God, I'm being such a coward. It's not any worse than being raped."

Malory couldn't keep his reaction to that off his face. He wanted to run out of the house and never bother Dave again. But that wasn't an option. He needed the man. So he sat stiffly waiting.

Dave reached across the table. "I didn't mean it that way. You're a friend. I could get used to being used by you, temporarily anyway." He forced a grin.

"Hey, that was a neat trick with the coffee."

Malory found a smile and pasted it on. "Thought you might appreciate that."

"Okay, so tell me your plan. One way or another, we've got to do this—for Rita—so I'm in. Whatever it takes."

"It's fairly simple. Once I locate the hit men, I'll lure them and their boss into my home. They'll come in the daylight expecting to kill me easily. But you and I'll be ready—and they'll die instead."

"You mean, you're going to use yourself as bait?"

"Yes."

"That must be like—like facing your worst nightmare."

"Yes. That's why I need you. These days, I've no other mortal friends I could trust for this."

"I'm ashamed. I shouldn't have hesitated to agree. Mal, do what you have to do so I can stand it. Don't let my squeamishness get in the way."

Malory rose, and Silver got up with him, glancing at the paling of the window. "I guess you've got to go."

"I was planning to stay here today. Remember the sanctuary I had built in your attic for Rita?"

"She never used it. I'd forgotten about it."

"With your permission...?"

"Well, sure. Are you afraid to go home?"

"It would be unwise. And I wished to be near you. Through your awareness, I can be roused, even during the day, if needed. Tonight, I'll check my security arrangements."

Malory went to the window and examined the yard by the rising light. He had to admit it out loud. He owed the man that much. "And, Dave, I've been bereaved often in my time, but rarely so deeply. I just don't want to be alone."

"I kinda feel the same way. Everybody else I know thinks she's been dead for years."

"She has been, Dave, she has been."

It went easier than Malory had expected. By the time he'd settled into the attic sanctuary, he'd adjusted his touch on Silver's mind to leave Silver with the feel of his presence without the impression of being violated.

By noon, it had become comfortable for both of them. By sundown, they'd worked out signals that would let Silver ask for privacy, and let Malory ask for admission. The link was clear and pure, like holding a private mental conversation. It had been centuries since Malory had worked with such an easy link. He'd miss it desperately when this was over.

Silver spent the day on the phone arranging to take his three weeks vacation instead of giving three weeks notice. And he'd followed the detailed instructions Malory had left for ordering the construction work.

When Malory rose, Silver was packed to move to Malory's house. Things were already in progress there. A decorator Malory'd used before had removed all the furniture from the living room and installed a large, carpeted pedestal in the center of the room, along with a grand piano in one corner, complete with silver candelabra.

The next day, workmen from a security contractor Malory relied on would rig the shutters on his living room windows—the huge bay windows overlooking the beach and Dave's house—to shut when weight came onto the floor near the pedestal.

When Malory woke, he called the undertaker he'd had "bury" Rita years ago, and ordered an ostentatious coffin to be delivered, black with a red satin lining. It would fit perfectly on the pedestal.

Late that night, visiting the security contractor at his home in San Jose, Malory carefully planted instructions to have the coffin altered. When the lid was raised by outside handles, an anesthetic spray would saturate the area. He also had invisible spy cameras placed all about the living room, the monitors banked in the bedroom just above it.

The automatic devices installed in the living room could also be controlled from a console in that bedroom. The console could also flood the lower floor with CO_2 foam. That console would be Silver's station during the days of waiting.

It was a long, tedious job to implant the details of the instructions then erase the memory of who'd given the orders. The workmen, he'd take care of as they finished their jobs.

With that done, Malory rechecked every sanctuary

he had installed around the Bay Area, every lookout he had planted at key locations near those sanctuaries, every point where any mortal might pick up a lead on his activities. But there was no hint that del Rio's people had found him.

Home about an hour before dawn, he went online to his brokerage house and opened an account for Silver, filing all the proper employee forms with the I.R.S. Then he activated the alternate identity he'd use when this was over. As an afterthought, he created an identity for Silver, too.

The following night, with preparations at his house progressing under Silver's guidance, Malory planted several threads connecting him to Rita, then began stalking his prey. He checked all del Rio's locations, infiltrating offices as mist, rifling files for names, dates, places, interrogating employees under compulsion, then erasing memories.

What he had expected to be a straightforward job turned into a tedious and unrewarding chore that dragged on and on and, as time passed, his hunger grew, his patience fled.

Three weeks after he'd found Rita charred and smoking, Malory slammed into the house and stalked into the living room. Dawn was graying the clear sky. Silver, disturbed by the sudden noise, came downstairs, tying his bathrobe. "Mal?"

Malory shouted, "Maybe it wasn't del Rio! Maybe I've been looking in the wrong place!"

Silver flinched.

Malory subsided. "I'm sorry. I've just become so used to feeding every night that this is getting on my nerves."

They both knew it was well past the time when Malory would have killed and feasted fully.

"Maybe," said Silver relaxing, "del Rio did away with those men so they wouldn't talk? Or he might have paid them off so well, they left the country." They'd kicked this idea around before, to no avail. Silver added, "If he paid them off, they're probably broke by now and on their way back."

"If he paid them off, there should be a record. I've been through their every record and most of their minds!"

"Have you?" Silver leaned against the gleaming black coffin. "Did you question del Rio himself?" Malory was silent. He'd been staying away from the top echelon to keep a low profile. Silver added, "What of his number-two men?"

"Women. Three of them, each running a division and reporting to del Rio. I questioned them. Nothing. They're not behind it. But del Rio...."

"If the killers were working directly for him, there wouldn't be records on any lower level. He wouldn't want it known he believes in vampires, would he? He wouldn't want his people to believe they're being stalked by a vampire."

That was a new thought. "You're right, Dave. Tomorrow, I'll confront del Rio, and if I still come up blank, I'll have to look at the other organizations around the Bay."

Malory's frustration subsided with that plan, and he looked around. The work had been completed and every bit of sawdust, every exposed wire, was gone. The bronze carpet was new, and so were the black drapes shielding the bay windows. All the new fabric had been fireproofed. The chemical stank.

Opening the windows, Malory said, "Get some deodorizer. The stage cobweb spray won't cover the odor of newness. When I do get them here, I don't want a false note to disrupt the illusion." He sat at the piano to play a bit of Chopin. The first chord he struck was sour. "And get the piano tuner in this afternoon. The number's on the rolodex in the kitchen. They'd never believe a vampire would have an untuned piano."

Swallowing his comment, Silver pulled his hand-held out of his robe pocket and made some entries in his task list and calendar.

Malory held out one hand. "Let me see that."

Silver folded the case open and handed it to him. Silver said, "It's just the same old one I use to note measurements for my clients. You've seen me use it."

Malory folded it up, noted the port where it could connect to a desk-top, then looked from it to Silver's robe pocket. "Maybe I haven't seen all the records! People carry these things around with them. And they don't think about them much." Absently, he handed it back as he rose. "Wake me an hour before sunset. It's going to be a busy night."

Silver's mental call came to Malory in his sanctuary cut into the rock of the hill under his house. The chamber was roughly four feet high by fifteen feet square, ventilated by a twenty yard long chimney not a half inch wide. It was his most secure location, because there was no entry a mortal could use. He had to turn to mist and sift through cracks in the rock or up the chimney. It had been difficult lining it with his native earth, and it had its own dangers. A quake could seal him in. Or Holy Water might miss the percolation layer and block the cracks so he couldn't use them.

He emerged into the windowless basement and dressed in the dark outfit Silver had laid out for him. Silver had tailored it to fit, making it of the flame-retardant fabric that Silver insisted he wear these days.

Using the mental link to learn if Silver had darkened the house, he emerged fighting grogginess, and went to his computer on the second floor. The shopping service yielded a comprehensive list of the pocket-sized palm sized computers currently available along with instructions for their use.

Malory was impressed. If he hadn't already possessed a perfect memory, he'd have ordered one for himself.

A little work with his maildrops, and he had del Rio's current location from his spies inside the gangster's organization, spies who would not remember dropping such notes.

Sternly putting aside his hunger, knowing it wasn't as bad as it felt, he headed for the living room intending to exit in batform through the chimney. He had just come through the archway, when Silver's pain lanced through him with paralyzing force, then subsided in an instant.

Malory forced his eyes open, berating himself for the lazy habit of maintaining the link with the mortal, and saw Silver bent double beside the window, holding his elbow and trying to breathe. In a flash, Malory was beside his friend.

Silver waved him off. "Nothing. I just hit my crazy bone. Be okay in a second."

But Malory saw the blood trickling through Silver's fingers. The blow had peeled off a flap of skin. He couldn't get his eyes off the ruby liquid. Then the smell took him.

Fighting it, moving in slow motion, he bent, hands coming out, tongue reaching, mouth opening. If he made contact, he'd be thrown into an unstoppable feeding frenzy.

Silver didn't understand. He'd gladly provided blood on occasion. He had no fear, and that was what ultimately saved him. As Malory sank into temptation, Silver shook Malory's shoulder. "Mal, your oath. Just wait a little longer."

Malory's eyes fixed on the mortal's and he got a fragile hold on himself, enough to stop but not to answer. Silver patted his shoulder, saying, "I'll put something on this."

Malory was left staring at his lack of reflection in the window, unable to remember what he'd looked like before. The hunger was worse than he'd thought. Tempted, he might take a kill now, breaking his vow, which could be fatal. Permanently fatal.

The gods of his fathers were unforgiving. Besides, succumbing to frenzy among the drug dealers could spook them. Then he'd never get Rita's killers. Struggling with the knowledge of his weakness, Malory was startled when Silver returned.

"Mal. I thought you'd be gone by now."

The wound was tightly covered with a plastic spray bandage and now Silver wore long sleeves. "Thank you, Dave. I've never owed a mortal such a large debt."

The man came across the carpet. He stopped more than arm's length from Malory, out of politeness, not fear, and offered, "We can call the debt square if you'd just answer, straight out, the questions you've always avoided."

"Questions?" Malory went to the window beside the bay window and finished opening it on the gathering fog aware of the thin smear of blood where Silver's elbow had impacted.

"I'm not a very good Jew, so if I don't think about it too much, I can see you as a bit foreign, or maybe an alien from outer space with powerful ESP. But turning into a bat, wolf, mist—no reflection, and an aversion for holy objects and flowing water—Mal, that's not alien. It's black magic!"

That gave Malory pause. "Magic?" He moved closer to Silver. "No. Magic is constrained by the laws of reality, same as science. I thought you understood, Dave. I was mortal once, a native creature of this earth. Now, I'm a supernatural creature, forced to stand half within and half without the laws of reality. The laws that constrain me are complex, and I've only just begun to understand them myself."

"But how did it happen? Who forced? Who constrained? Why?" He gestured at the casket. "I know you're just playing on human fears with this nonsense, but they say people become vampires by making a deal with the Devil."

"The Devil? No, not in my case." He'd never told any mortal before, but Silver had demanded payment. "A god cursed me, a legitimate god to whom I'd been promised as a sacrifice before I was born."

Silver gaped. He hardly had to say it. Malory could read his face and didn't need to check his mind. Pagan gods weren't real. They were made up by ignorant people. With incredible naïveté, Silver answered, "But human sacrifice is immoral. How could you be blamed for refusing?"

"I didn't refuse," Malory snapped, offended. "Dave, long before the Creator of the Universe came to Abram the son of Terah, He made me the same offer. But my father had promised me to our god at my birth. After all what else were third sons of a king good for? So I hesitated.

"Our god was angry that I'd think to abandon my destiny, and cursed me to consume only human blood and to perish in the light of the sun. The curse came on me that very night. The power of our god was real, and there was an army about to besiege our city. I was to be sacrificed to save us from sack and ruin. It was my duty. I told the Creator of the Universe, that I wouldn't go anywhere but to my sacrifice.

"My god wouldn't accept the sacrifice of my life because after the ritual, I didn't stay dead. The Creator had denied my city the sacrifice needed to survive the war. But He gave me the powers I needed to survive my god's curse. He said I must witness the working out of His blessing on the one who would accept it. So far all I've seen is periodic slaughter of the descendants of Abram. I'm still devoted to the god of my fathers, so I have problems with holy things dedicated to the Creator. The Devil has absolutely nothing to do with it."

Silver's bushy black eyebrows rose to disappear under his cowlick. "You've spoken...with...God?"

It was the tone one typically used with a suspected nut case. "Maybe not," assured Malory. "Maybe that's how I remember it, because someone tampered with my mind. It never happened again. I've been on my own for millennia, trying to fathom the laws of my existence. One thing I'm certain of—the best way for me to avoid personal disaster is to eliminate my daughter's killer. And to keep the vow to my god."

Silver digested all that silently, then nodded. "I think I understand better now." To Malory's astonishment, he actually seemed relieved. "Well, you'd better get going if you're going to confront del Rio tonight."

He watched as Malory took the turning step that twisted him through another dimension, leaving only a small bat form as his manifestation in the human reality stratum. For the first time in millennia, Malory was acutely conscious of a peaceful sort of pleasure in the shift, a sharp contrast to the effect of taking life's blood or exposure to sunlight. There was a very great difference between the two gods.

Still, the god of his fathers was not to be ignored.

This night, del Rio was working out of a new, well-kept warehouse on the Embarcadero. Already the fog horns were blasting their warnings. It made fine cover for any noise.

Malory folded his bat form under the eaves over a well lit office window and extended his senses. A freighter was tied up at the wharf nearby, reeking of cocaine. Neither police dogs nor mechanical sniffers seemed able to detect drugs the way a vampire could.

Six men in the office were closing a deal over the delivery, del Rio and two guards facing three strangers.

Malory listened for hours and learned nothing until the strangers left. Del Rio turned to a guard. "Get Dillon and Petrino back from Cancun. I've got a job for them."

"They might not come. You shouldn't pay 'em so well."

"I pay what a job's worth. That's why they'll come."

The guard left mumbling that nothing could be worth that kind of money. Malory's heart raced. Dillon and Petrino could be the ones who'd killed Rita.

With growing impatience, Malory waited for del Rio to be left alone. It was close to midnight before things settled down and del Rio put his feet up on his desk, popping the top on a beer can. He seemed to be waiting for something, but Malory decided to risk it. He'd only need a few minutes.

He launched himself into the air, twisted into a rope of fine mist, and glided through the hairline crack under the window. He took control of del Rio's mind as he formulated himself before the desk. He could never have entered del Rio's own home, but this was a public space, an office.

Shocked, del Rio jerked once, trying to drive his hand toward the signal button under his desk. Then he subsided in the grip of Malory's mind.

He was a short, stocky man with a touch of distinguished frosting at his temples. His skin was dusky, his hair black. His nose had been broken in two places, and there was a v-shaped nick in the top of his right ear.

Gripping his mind lightly, Malory studied the man, waiting for him to recover from shock. He'd never laid eyes on him before, but he knew him intimately. He was quick, sharp and ruthless. In the last three years, he'd ordered more deaths in the Bay Area than any other importer.

At last, del Rio asked, "Who are you?"

"The father of the vampire you had killed."

Malory watched del Rio's mind grind through memories of terror as the mysterious deaths in his ranks spooked his finest operators. Then came the eyewitness account of a vampire leaving a warm corpse. That was himself, Malory realized. Del Rio's men had threatened to defect *en masse* if del Rio didn't stop the vampire.

Del Rio had set a trap, sacrificing an untrustworthy messenger. Rita had fallen into the trap. While video cameras had failed to record Rita's presence, her victim's gyrations and death were recorded. Meanwhile, a sketch artist had caught Rita's likeness perfectly.

With del Rio's connections, a portrait was all he needed to run down an individual as fast as the police could.

So Rita had paid for all her victims as well as for Malory's. If Malory had fallen into the trap, things might have gone differently. "I want the tape," said Malory.

Del Rio didn't hedge. He knew exactly what tape, and, shaking, he produced it from a desk drawer. As he bent, Malory saw the edge of a case in the man's impeccably tailored pocket. In a lightning swift move, Malory had it in his own hand. It was indeed a handheld like Silver's but much larger.

He took videotape and handheld, saluted courteously, and then, just as a man ushered another into the room, Malory ostentatiously turned into a bat, twisting the tape and diary through into the other dimension because a bat could never lift the weight in reality and flew to the window, where he turned to mist and sifted out the way he'd come.

Before leaving, he paused to get a good impression of their reactions. Ghastly, white-face shock followed by sheer terror. Simultaneously, both del Rio and his guest realized that the organization's most private and sensitive records were now in the vampire's hands.

At last, the guest declared, "You'll bring me proof that you've retrieved or destroyed those records, or no one will ever deal with you again." He stalked from the room, a picture of power and dignity despite the inner knowledge that he'd wet his pants.

Del Rio remained sitting at his desk with similar knowledge, and he didn't rise until the last of those he'd issued orders to had left.

Malory departed certain that del Rio would soon put Rita's killers, and most probably himself, into Malory's trap.

It was almost sunrise.

While he and Silver were spraying stage cobwebs in the kitchen, Silver asked, "What if del Rio brings an army?"

"He won't. It could prove too...embarrassing if word got around that del Rio is crazy, possibly from using his own product. What else would anyone think who saw him pounding a stake through someone's heart? Besides, word would certainly get out that his private records had been stolen. No, he's got to retrieve that handheld secretly. He'll use the only two hit men he has who've been successful against a vampire, and they'll use that same successful technique."

"Unsuccessfully." He led the way into the living room.

Malory circled the casket. "Yes." He laid a hand

on the ebony surface. "Dave, this is your last chance to back out. I'm going to feast on those men. It will be ugly, and I may not be able to prevent you from observing it all."

He shook his head decisively. "I've thought through what you told me last evening. I'm in."

"You could be killed."

"Rita was killed. I'm in. You can't deny my right."

"No. I can't." He eyed the graying fog. "Secure the house, then. I'll sleep in the casket today. But I think it will take them more than one day to find me."

"Probably. But if you'd told them any more than that you were associated with Rita, they'd have figured it was a trap. Now they'll have to work through reams of computer records and check out everyone she dealt with to find you. Shoot, they might end up at my house first!"

Malory raised the casket lid carefully not using the trick handles. "The cost of damage to your property would easily be covered by the funds I've put in your name."

"That sounds awfully final."

"I doubt my existence is threatened, but Malory Avnel must disappear after the confrontation, and this house will no doubt become useless to me." At Silver's stricken look, he assured, "It's a small loss. I've others." He closed the lid, settling down with only a thread of contact to Silver.

Three days passed, four, five, and nothing. The strict fast tightened around Malory's guts. He spent the days in restless vigilance, and the nights pacing, watching his clocks tick off the hours of his fast.

On the sixth night, he was tempted to return to del Rio and give him a clue. Surely, the man wasn't so incompetent.

But Silver talked him out of it, speculating that the hit men might not have returned from Cancun so quickly, or that they were preparing weapons. "Be prepared for buckets of Holy Water, and dozens of consecrated crosses. They can buy priests down in South America. How about consecrated Host? What can we do to defend against anything like that?"

"Let them believe I'm more helpless than I am. Unless they bring a priest to administer these weapons, the effect will be mild. After all, consider the sins on *their* souls."

"I didn't know that made a difference."

"It does." But it set him to thinking, and later that night, when Silver had gone to sleep, Malory performed a ritual he hadn't thought about in millennia, consecrating the house itself to the service of his god, burying sacred symbols before the windows and doors, carving signs into the concrete. Now, the purest and most devout wielder of Jewish, Christian, or Moslem objects wouldn't be a real threat.

His efforts had an odd side-effect. For the next two nights, he didn't feel moment by moment that he was about to break his vow. In the day, he rested better, less tormented.

They came on the bright, sunny eighth morning.

Malory knew it even before Silver alerted him by knocking on his mind. "Mal, there's someone in the garden."

He fought his way to the edge of consciousness, the weight of day like lead on his chest. "It's them, the two who exposed Rita. I recognize their, well, minds." The psychic flavor, like the scent of a specific perfume worn by a specific person, was identical.

He could feel Silver swallowing hard. "Right. Then where's del Rio? You said he'd come personally."

"But taking the least risk. You mustn't do anything until del Rio is inside the house with the other two."

"I know the plan."

To Malory's consternation, he dozed off, waiting. Only Silver's frantic mental nudging brought him awake. "They're in the garage! Are they going to blow up the cars?"

Now that was a possibility they hadn't planned on. But Malory didn't think that was it. Too chancy.

There was another long wait and Malory faded in and out under the weight of daylight, Silver fretting ever more at how groggy the vampire was.

And then Malory sensed it, just a whiff filtered through the mortal's crude senses, but no mistaking the pungency. "Dave, it's garlic. They've flooded the heating system with garlic. The heat's on, isn't it?"

"Yes. It was cold when I got up."

"Well, turn it off!"

If Malory had been alone, this would have been ineffective. He never used heat except to prevent mildew.

Very quickly, the scent turned to a thick miasma, a cloying solidity in the air. Malory had to shut down his link to the mortal for his own distress was growing.

Malory had seen to it that the casket wasn't air tight, so he could emerge as mist through a tiny hole in the side.

Now, he noticed the hole he'd made was on a line with the breeze from a heating vent. He shoved his elbow against the hole. In dormancy, he wasn't breathing much, but still the scent was paralyzing. He fought to regain contact with Silver and found the human frantically trying to get his attention. "They're on the roof!"

Seeking the killers, Malory realized they were doing something to his chimney. He'd never used the fireplace that occupied one wall of the living room, but he did often use the chimney in mist or bat form.

He had to look through Silver's squinting, watery eyes at one of the living room monitors to see what came down that shaft, but he recognized it before Silver. "Censer! Bigger than they'd use in a cathedral. Looks like a custom job."

Smoke billowed from the incense burner, pouring out through the holes around the cross-shaped carvings in the sides. Even from inside the casket, Malory could feel the thing vibrating with the peculiar tone of The Creator. And the smoke! The incense had been specially blessed. Silver's words echoed through his mind. *They can buy priests.*

Though Malory's consecrations of his window and door sills were not wholly effective, they cut the impact of the sacred smoke by half, and it had already been vitiated by the impiety of the wielders. But Malory was still weakened and distracted from the garlic and misery mounted fast.

He'd never understood his antipathy to garlic, except that certain sacred herbs and woods did have massive effects on him. Right now, he wasn't interested in understanding.

"Dave, go up to the third floor." There were three empty bedrooms up there. "On the wall by the thermostat, there's a switch like a lightswitch, but it's black with a plain black plate around it. It's an attic fan. Turn it on." It hadn't been cleaned or oiled since before he'd moved in. Nobody needed such a thing in a house overlooking the Pacific. "Hurry, Dave, they'll be up to something else soon."

The mortal was already on his way when Malory sensed a shift in the air-pressure. He had located the two invaders at the kitchen windows, overlooking the little enclosed garden. He deduced they'd just cut their way in through the window. They'd be climbing in over the sink now, probably using the ladder they'd taken from the garage. Obviously, they'd spent the last few days carefully casing the house.

Just then, the attic fan thundered to life. With only the chimney, the stove hood, and now the kitchen window open, the powerful fan must be drawing gustily. Malory sensed the invaders' surprise.

As Silver raced back down the stairs, his steps covered by the vibration of the fan, Malory told him,

"They're in the kitchen. If they start a fire, cut that fan!"

"It's helping the garlic."

And the incense. But as the frightening effect of the smells abated, Malory found himself dozing again, too lethargic to care about the killers heading for the casket in which he lay.

He was shocked out of it when a sound like a sluicing downpour engulfed him, and he abruptly felt cut off from the outside world, suffocating (though he was barely breathing).

"Dave!"

"They're using something like fire extinguishers to spray something onto the coffin from way over by the doorway. They're really afraid of you. Look through my eyes."

It felt like the mortal was a million miles away. "I can't take your eyes. It's Holy Water." By the gallon, just as Dave had predicted.

A thin, shivering thought invaded Malory's mind. Could he trust Dave after telling him that he'd refused the offer of the God of Abraham? Had Silver made a deal with Rita's killers? Or was he just better at thinking like a modern man than Malory was?

"I'm going to flood the room in CO_2 foam," said Silver.

"No!" commanded Malory. "They don't know about you. Let them get close to the casket and try to open it."

But the two men circled the room and went out the

arch toward the front door, pausing every so often to nail up a silver cross. The house vibrated with queer discomfort.

In moments, the front door opened and del Rio himself, clad in what looked like a NASA isolation suit, entered carrying a doctor's bag. Standing in the living room entry, he examined the stage setting, face set in a wooden mask. But Malory could hear the man's heart skip and race.

Malory couldn't help but admire the mortal. His knuckles were white on the doctor's bag, but his step was firm as he circled the casket, checked out the piano by striking middle C, swiped at the cobweb festooning the candelabra, then yanked the black draperies away from the windows. Malory knew sunlight streamed into the room.

Everywhere del Rio stepped, everywhere he touched, the power of the Holy Water diminished a bit. His confidence built until he swaggered up to the coffin and his weight triggered the slam of the steel roll shutters over the windows.

Swallowing in a dry throat, del Rio ran his hand over the casket, admiring the quality. To Malory, it was as if del Rio's sin-blackened touch ripped a strip out of the Holy Water seal plastered to his coffin. Immediately, all of Malory's senses broke free.

The vampire took his first free breath since the deluge and relaxed. "Dave, just sit tight."

"You're back! The curtains are open! But the shutters are closed. Let me flood the place."

Malory swathed Silver's mind in firm control, damping his panic. He watched through the monitors as del Rio set his bag on top of the casket, laid it open and extracted a thermal pot filled with clay or wax, soft enough to mold.

It was quite a large pot. Having never seen such a thing before, Malory couldn't imagine what it was. Then, through the tiny hole in the side of the casket, he caught the faintest whiff, beeswax, and suddenly he knew.

Alarm thrilled along his nerves, followed by black terror that paralyzed his thinking.

Dave, through the grip Malory had on his mind, was likewise frozen in shock. Not knowing why, he tried to reassure the vampire. "They're going to make a waxworks duplicate of your features! I've seen it done in Paris."

Yet even as Silver spoke, del Rio slapped lumps of the wax over the latch where the coffin would open and then in three places on the crack, saying, "He might not be in here. Soon as this is done, we'll search the rest of the place." From his bag, he produced a large stick with a disk on one end. He drove the disk against a blob of wax. A seal.

Malory screamed in agony, and del Rio chuckled.

Crosses, Malory could have dealt with, but this was a five pointed star, the lines over counterclockwise. The symbol had been used by Jews and later by Christians and even Moslems, but it was in fact, much older than that.

As each seal slammed into place, Malory envisioned uncounted centuries imprisoned in this coffin. Panic took him, followed by rage. As del Rio struck the final blow printing the star on the last blob of wax, Malory remembered his exit hole, sealed only by Holy Water.

Twisting himself into mist, Malory forced his way through the hole, feeling the lingering resistance like a static field disrupting his nerves. As he formulated in the room, his knees were daytime weak. Light coming through the arches seared his eyes, and his skin crawled even under the factor thirty sunblock.

But he faced Rita's killers across the casket, and still managed to use Dave's hands to trigger the anesthetic gas. It couldn't touch del Rio in his isolation suit, but it would take out the two killers.

The instant they saw the billowing fog erupt from the base of the pedestal, they whipped gas masks off their belts and slipped them over their heads. There were crosses on the masks. One of them had a crossbow armed with a silver tipped bolt of rowan wood. The other retreated toward the kitchen, not with panic, but fading slowly back behind his covering partner, probably intent on bringing forth another weapon.

Behind the mask of the environment suit, del Rio's face was pale, but carved in wood again. Despite the airtight seals, Malory felt he could smell the man's fear. His voice, however, was steady as he said, "I came for my notepad. Give it to me, and I won't bother you again."

"You ordered my daughter killed."

"She was killing my men. Since she died, I haven't lost any more. As long as things stay that way, I won't bother you or your kind again. Just give me my notepad."

Upstairs, Silver's agitation was growing as he bent over the monitor showing the kitchen. The other killer was priming some sort of pump with a hose attached. More Holy Water? Malory ignored him. The crossbow was more dangerous.

Prepared to twist into mist if the archer fired, the vampire said, "Her death was extremely unpleasant. I won't make any effort to cushion yours."

As he spoke, he carefully withdrew control from Silver and wove his way into the archer's mind, taking control first of his speech centers, then his hands, and the rest.

Del Rio replied, "You do realize I've got you trapped? You can't escape from this house."

Malory shifted the bowman's weight and let him pivot slowly, hoping del Rio wouldn't notice the movement.

"Listen, Avnel, or whatever you call yourself, just give me back my property, and I'll let you go."

Malory used his proxy hands to fire the crossbow right into del Rio's throat. Blood spurted. But Malory wasn't watching. With the preternatural swiftness of his kind, he leaped over the casket and launched himself at the archer. With one hand he wrenched the cross from around the man's neck. His sharp teeth ripped into the killer's throat. They hit the carpet, but

Malory didn't feel it.

Blood spurted from the carotid artery into Malory's parched mouth, and ecstasy took him. He lost awareness of everything but sucking and swallowing. Warmth flowed into his belly, his limbs came alive, his skin began to feel. Surge after surge of pure power flowed into him, making him ache for more, holding and holding him to his prey.

He came out of it only when bright flame licked at his eyelids. In reflex, he rolled off his victim, and in one motion was on his feet.

A sheet of flame cut the room in half while a voice on the other side of the flame cried, "Mr. del Rio! This way!"

But del Rio was busy bleeding to death.

CO_2 foam flooded down from the ceiling. Malory had felt Silver hit the control a moment before the automatics cut in. Silver would have reacted faster, the vampire realized, but for watching his professed friend in the throes of a feeding frenzy. And Malory was still hungry.

With the foam damping the flames, he advanced on the man with the flamethrower, his movements fueled by fresh blood, and the promise of more. As he closed, knocking the nozzle out of the way, the flames spewed again, engulfing the archer's body, sending up a stench of cooking meat. Malory wrenched the flame thrower away and tore the man's throat out.

The silver cross singed his skin, but he hardly felt it as fresh, rich blood glided down his throat. The sere rawness at the back of his nose was eased at last by the fumes of blood, fresh, warm, thick, living blood. And there was pure rapture in fulfilling his vow to his god, a relief that the danger of becoming forsworn was over.

The man was dead when Malory raised his head at last, hazily realizing the house was on fire. That last burst with the flamethrower had flamed the beams above the ceiling. Smoke filled the room despite the layer of foam on the floor, burying del Rio's white environment suit.

Malory bent, brushing foam aside. Del Rio was still alive. He ripped the suit fabric, surprised the tough synthetic parted so easily. *No,* he realized, *I've regained his strength.* He shook the man to awareness to be sure he knew what was happening. Then he sucked the remaining life from him.

He hadn't needed it, but it was satisfying nonetheless.

Only then did his attention turn to Silver. He realized the mortal had gone to the third floor to turn off the attic fan after he'd triggered the CO_2. Now he was trapped in a bedroom, stuffing the cracks under the door with rags and newspaper, unable to climb down from the third floor window.

"Mal!" his thought squealed when Malory made his presence felt. "Get out! Call the fire department!"

"No. The bodies have to burn completely." He pulled the crossbow bolt from del Rio's neck, took up the flame thrower and immolated the three corpses, taking care that the neck tissue charred. There would still be plenty of evidence for the police, but his nature would not be revealed.

The fire was rapidly sweeping upwards in the building, no doubt setting off smoke detectors in the adjacent houses. With the smoke too thick to see, Malory found a dark closet where, shielded from the sun, he turned to bat form. Keeping well above the flames, he flew up the smoky stairwell.

He had to get Silver out of the house. But he had no idea how to get him down the stairs. *Has to be down the outside—in sunlight. I can do it.* He couldn't face the prospect of losing his new friend now.

At the third floor, he found Silver's room, turned to mist and filtered through the rags stuffed under the door. Formulating, he squinted against the terrible sunlight.

Silver jumped. "Hhhuh! Oh. How did you get up here?"

"Flew."

For the first time, Silver shrank from Malory, and it hurt more than Malory wanted to think about when the mortal asked hesitantly, "You aren't still hungry, are you?"

"No, but it wouldn't matter if I were. You're safe from me, Dave. You helped me keep an oath I dared not break." He edged up to the window to get his bearings. Then he sensed it. On the outside of the window-sill, a blob of wax with a five pointed star. It was on top of the god-sign he'd etched there.

He leaned against the wall, one forearm over his

head. He could wait out the fire in his stone sanctuary. When the ashes cooled, the seals that were no doubt on all the doors and windows, even the chimney, would no longer be effective. But he couldn't get out this window now. So he couldn't carry Silver out the window and down the wall.

Silver eyed the door. Smoke was seeping through the rags and around the top. He was still getting most of Malory's thoughts directly.

He looked at the windowsill and saw the wax seal. At once, he began to lift the window. Malory stopped him. "Draft will pull the fire into the room."

"But way before that, I'll have that seal off of there and you can get out and maybe get us both down." The window squealed up and Silver leaned out to scrape the wax off. His arm recoiled as if he'd touched a coal. "Ah! It's hot!"

Malory cut the link with Silver. "Try again."

Silver got a paint stick from a pile of trash in the corner and leaned out to scrape the wax. The stick flew from his hands, spinning down. "God! What is that thing?"

"Seal of Solomon. It's aimed at me, but you're so tightly involved with me now that it's got you, too. We can't erase it because we didn't set it. And those who did are dead."

"I'm going to die in here."

"No!" commanded Malory.

"Promise me, Mal, promise you won't make me over. If this is death, I accept it. At least we got those bastards."

"You've had my word on that for years." He could hear the flames roaring and crackling in the central stairwell. Soon it would be too late for him to go down. Even his mist form couldn't penetrate open flame.

Silver began to cough on the smoke drawn into the room by the open window.

Malory slammed the window and took off his jacket to stuff it under the door, but it wouldn't fold. The hand-held was in the breast pocket. He took it out, weighing it in one hand while he kicked the jacket under the door. It weighed at least ten times what his bat form weighed. Yet he'd transported the thing across the city.

For all his millennia of sporadic scholarship, he'd never found a clue as to how he did what he did. It had been centuries since he'd discovered a new ability. But it had been centuries since he'd really needed a new skill.

He tossed the thing from hand to hand.

"That can't get us out of this. Go, Mal. Flame can kill you, permanently."

He looked at Silver, really looked. He couldn't remember ever having a friend quite like this one before. He didn't want to remember for millennia to come that he'd let him die out of sheer cowardice.

"I've got an idea, but it's dangerous. It might leave you certifiable; it might kill us both, but it might work."

"Let's hear it," Silver said, but Malory heard the reservation. He'd rather die than let Malory risk death to save him. Fire sirens wailed in the distance.

"Maybe I can carry you the way I carry my clothes—or small objects like this. I've never tried it with a person, before. I just assumed it wouldn't work. It might not."

"I don't understand. Exactly what would happen?"

"I don't know. I don't know how I do it." He paced, fretfully. The floor was getting warm. "There's another place where things wait while what's left of me here moves. When I get where I'm going, I just *turn* everything out and reformulate myself. I might not be able to turn you into that place, or maybe I won't be able to move if I do, or maybe I won't be able to reformulate you because you're about equivalent to my own mass. Or I might even find I can't reformulate myself. I don't know how it works!"

"I don't like it." Malory knew he was about to reject the idea totally, to accept death, when a gout of flame shot up from the corner of the room closest to the living room.

Silver jumped, moving toward Malory, and the vampire stepped into and around the mortal, scooping him up in his arms and completing his turn into mist.

It seemed to take forever and ever. Very gradually, he became dimly conscious of his focal point in the mist, and the vast drag of Silver's panic somewhere else.

He hovered in the midst of the burning room, struggling with Silver's panic, groping for his mind. At last, he found the mortal consciousness and wrestled it down to darkness.

Then he could move. Laboriously, he slipped through the crack at the top of the door. The hall was aflame. He could, however, manage to ride the cool currents, for as the warmed air from the fire rose, the colder air from the top of the house literally poured down the stairs.

The trip was a nightmare, dodging, rising, falling out of control, being inexorably pushed this way and that. It was like staggering under a massive load, careening out of control in a hurricane wind.

Toward the end, Malory knew he had failed and was about to die a final death, his mist form evaporated by tongues of flame. On the ground floor, he barely avoided catastrophe for the fifth time, and raged inwardly. Here he was trying to save the mortal life of one of the best of Abram's descendants, and the Creator of the Universe couldn't spare a flicker of mercy for the guy. *So I'm glad I didn't accept Your offer if this is how you'd have treated my descendants!* And he swore in several extinct languages.

With one last spiteful effort, he filtered into his rocky sanctuary. Still mist, he rested, feeling scorched and weak enough to weep. *What if I can't do it?*

Listen, prayed the vampire in his mother tongue, *I'm sorry for what I said. There are a whole lot more descendants of Abram now than there were total humans alive in his own time. You've made a good start on your promise. But don't you think maybe Dave here could help increase that number, with just a bit of your help now?*

For a long time, the vampire rested, gathering strength for the *turn* that would restore Silver's body, if not maybe his mind. Then, with the last dregs of his strength, he heaved them both around that indescribable corner.

"Mal!" screamed Silver in terror at the pitch darkness.

Malory rolled over to drag one infinitely heavy arm across Silver's chest. "Relax, we're in my sanctuary. It's solid rock, remember? The fire can't get us here."

"It worked? It worked! My God!"

"Yes. Your God. Definitely the more powerful." *I think.* Once he knew Silver had survived physically and mentally, Malory's thoughts unraveled under the powerful daytime lethargy. "I'll wake at sundown, then we'll leave. Sleep, Dave, you've earned it."

TRUE DEATH

"Chelsea won that lawsuit!"

"What lawsuit?"

"The one to keep Saint Germain."

David Silver waved the hardcover book he was reading. "This is a new one!"

Malory Avnel had come to relish Silver's cryptic greetings in the months since the mob had destroyed his house in San Francisco. But dawn was approaching, and Malory's patience was thin.

Gently, he closed the window he'd just flown through. Silver had thoughtfully left the window open to save him the trouble of reformulating as mist and sifting through the cracks. He flicked the air on, then strode across the apartment's neutral-toned Ethan Alan living room to the white and gold painted mantel that concealed his own door, replying absently, "I'm glad he won his lawsuit, but I thought church and state were separate."

"She. Chelsea Quinn Yarbro. Saint Germain is a fictional vampire based on the real historical Saint Germain. But he wasn't a saint. That's just his name."

The word *vampire* caught Malory's attention. Silver

was stretched out in his recliner. His book had a glossy indigo cover and red lettering. *Better in the Dark.*

Silver looked up, scrutinizing Malory. "Okay, so Saint Germain wasn't really a vampire and you could pick holes in the historical depictions because you were there while she only researched it. That's not the point. I wanted to see what it feels like to live through so many millennia; how human behavior never changes, which makes boredom the biggest threat to the will to—what's wrong, Mal?"

"I've had a hard night. I came in thinking I could use some lackluster routine for a change. And I find you so excited about boredom that you've stayed up all night reading about it."

Silver looked at his book as if he'd never seen it before. "But it's a love sto—" Silver broke off and set the book on the lamp stand. He pushed up out of the recliner. Coming toward Malory with one hand out, he said, "I just read this stuff for fun. If it bothers you—"

"I enjoy your fun; I enjoy your sharing your fun with me, even when it involves fictional vampires. I wish I had something equally pleasurable to share with you." He intercepted Silver's hand before it landed on his shoulder.

"Ah," said Silver. "You don't want to talk about what's bothering you." Silver's grip on Malory's hand and conveyed acceptance of that reluctance.

"Tonight will be soon enough." Malory returned the grip and dropped the warm, human hand.

"Then there is something bothering you."

"Yes!" Malory snapped. "It's almost dawn." He triggered the hidden mechanism. As the panel swung inward, he sighed. "Sorry. I'll see you tonight."

Silver opened his mouth for another delaying comment, but the fax machine bleeped. "I'll get that. Sleep well."

Silver turned toward the bedroom they used for an office and Malory stepped into the anteroom of his sleeping chamber. "I will." He triggered the panel shut, leaving him in cool darkness. The inner door, which would shield him from sunlight should anyone open the outer door during the day, swung silently at a touch. Air conditioning kept it dry enough in this windowless chamber to prevent mold.

When they had arrived in Miami, they had moved into this manager's suite of this apartment building. The entire lower floor of this upscale building had been built by one of Malory's aliases and was now owned by another. The suite had been constructed around the fire-proof retreat Malory required. Silver's rooms surrounded that protected core. For months now, Silver had managed both the apartment building and Malory's daytime affairs with growing confidence.

Watching the little tailor blossom into a computer nerd and Mutual Fund Maven via GEnie and E-mail had restored Malory's zest for life. But the human's recent choice in reading matter was worrisome.

As the vampire disrobed and settled in his curtained bed, he regretted his promise to stay out of Silver's mind. The mortal had surely earned his privacy with his assistance against the killers of Malory's youngest "daughter," Rita. But it would have been reassuring to know what was going on in Silver's mind.

He surrendered to the rising sun, bemused by the collage of fragmented memories swirling through his thoughts. From San Francisco, they had driven across country in a van equipped for Malory's daytime requirements. As Silver recovered from the shock of his first close encounter with the darker side of magic and the supernatural, the mortal had begun to edit his world view. Many night drives were punctuated with whirlwind conversations about religion, magic, and the difference between magic and the supernatural creatures such as Malory.

When they'd moved into the apartment, Silver had surprised, and offended, Malory by affixing a mezuzah to the doorpost to his bedroom. Silver had never placed credence in the trappings of his religion until he'd seen the effectiveness of Malory's invocations while fighting the vampire hunters in San Francisco. Suddenly, the tailor had troubled to obtain a truly kosher mezuzah and affix it with due ceremony, including a recitation of the appropriate blessing in stumbling but effective Hebrew.

Malory had wakened that evening with an eerie sensation, somewhere between a bad smell and insects crawling over his skin. Then he'd discovered he was unable to enter Silver's bedroom, even upon invitation. Silver was astonished at the effect on Malory, and Malory was astonished that Silver had been able to produce the effect.

"I could take it down," Silver had offered hesitantly. "I didn't mean to bar you, just, well...."

"No. That's all right. I'll get used to it. And if it makes you feel safer, there's no harm in it."

"It's your apartment, after all—"

"And it's your bedroom. Just...don't put up any more of them. All right?"

Silver hadn't put up any more, but it had taken months for Malory to adjust to that subliminal hum, discordant itch, or whatever it was. It wasn't inimical to his being, after all. The Potency that enabled the mezuzah was the very same Potency that had endowed him with virtual immortality so he could observe the fate of Abram's get.

The clashing vibration was caused by the objection of his own god, the god of his father's city, the god to whom he'd been sacrificed, the god who had cursed him with the need for blood and darkness. He had died but his city's god had rejected the sacrifice because, through no will of his own, Malory hadn't stayed dead.

Every so often, throughout the millennia, Malory found his simplest daily affairs tied into complex knots because he was the bone of contention between two such potencies.

Blurring into daytime dormancy, Malory thought that the arrival of David Silver in his life may turn out to be the harbinger of truly monumental complications. But it wasn't Silver's fault. He alone had invoked divine attention.

Around noon, Malory's awareness rippled with Silver's presence, the only presence able to enter his chamber without setting off alarms that could waken him even in daylight. The residual thread connecting their minds reassured Malory that Silver was busy, intent, but undisturbed, unalarmed, and certainly posing no threat to a lethargic vampire.

Malory sank back into his stupor, filled with renewed anxiety. The changes in the tailor's attitudes were especially alarming in view of recent developments.

I'll just have to explain to him and ask to access his mind again. If Silver denied him, they would part company. The mortal had served him well. He could not violate Silver's trust, nor allow himself or his affairs to become a danger to the mortal. With that decision, peace came at last and he slept.

When Malory woke, he was already half-way onto his feet, intent on carrying out his decision as if not one instant had passed, yet now it was dusk, and his energies, the gift of the god of his fathers, not the God of Abram, waxed steadily with the night.

A single piece of yellow paper fluttered to the floor at his feet, a large Post-It note that had come unstuck from his nightshirt. He retrieved Silver's note and flicked on the dim night light he used in lieu of candles.

"The plumber fixed the toilets. They don't spew hot water anymore. I filed for damages. I bought two thousand more of VWINX because it's the best Vanguard Fund. CNBC says the bear will be a grizzly. I posted the gardener's job. And I paid the GEnie bill. Both my

VCR's are taping. The one in the living room is free though. I left your surveillance camera tape on top. If you need me, I'll be at the Hyatt downtown, probably until midnight. I heard on GEnie that P. N. Elrod is reading at a convention there and I just couldn't resist. I know you needed to talk, so I'll be back around one."

It was a typical David-Silver-Post-It, but something about the handwriting made Malory uneasy. He worried at it as he dressed and went out to tour the apartment.

According to post-its on the VCR's, Silver was taping Highlander and Forever Knight, whatever they were. The empty red BASF boxes on top of the sets had old TV Guide clippings taped to them. It appeared that Highlander was about an immortal and Forever Knight had something to do with a vampire cop. *Research. Via fiction.* This was becoming serious.

Silver had rejected all offers of immortality for himself. So what was he after? If something, perhaps a demon, was luring him on in this research, Silver might already be a victim of force he could never handle.

Galvanized, Malory rushed into the office and powered up the desktop. As he waited, he noticed a disk in a wrapper with the title *The Vampire's Crypt*, edited by a Margaret Carter from someplace in Maryland. It offered interviews with female writers and extensive bibliographies.

Silver had left the referenced item from GEnie so it came right up on screen. Scanning the text, Malory learned two things. P. N. Elrod was another female writer of vampire novels. A quick check of the source of the item revealed that her fans were legion, and many of them were articulate females. She'd been interviewed in Vampire's Crypt, and reviewed in a thing called The Monthly Aspectarian. Astrology was definitely not a David Silver interest. Alarmed, Malory shut the machine down.

As he reformulated into bat-shape, he did consider that he could be misinterpreting Silver's interests. It had been almost a year since Rita had died, and maybe two since she had chosen immortality over marrying Silver. It was time for Silver to be interested in women again. Perhaps he was looking for one who wouldn't reject Malory's position in Silver's new life. *No, he's not that naive.*

Malory arrived at the Hyatt, riding the formidable evening gusts above the tallest spires rather than using his supernatural powers to relocate. If this was the demon's trap, he wouldn't advertise his approach. And what better bait for a vampire trap than David Silver? What better bait for Silver than vampire lore? It was just the way Malory's god would think. And his god had taken no vow to eschew influencing Silver's mind.

Don't spook yourself!

But the previous night, Malory had thought he'd glimpsed Xlrud, his god's favorite demon servant, and he had indeed been tensed and waiting for something to happen. *And this is it. It's Xlrud playing on Silver's innate curiousity.*

Malory landed in the darkest shadows behind an

airport limo idling beside the valet parking sign. He swirled into human form, and tucked in his Aeropostale polo shirt. Costumed in white Dockers and Reeboks, he lacked only the sun-scorched look of the early-retired executive so typical of Florida. Still, he'd blend in with the Hyatt guests.

He strode through the carriage entrance, ignored by the bellhops. A rush of voices filled the hollow towering space over the lobby. Scaffolds and spackled drop cloths denoted recent remodeling. The escalator was in pieces and deserted. Following the signs to the Registration desk, Malory found himself approaching a knot of grungily attired people, the source of the noise competing with the tall fountain.

They milled about the display showing daily events. He leaned against a fake Doric column where he would seem to belong to a loaded luggage cart and observed the crowd.

These people wore myriads of slogan buttons and carried totebags plastered with cryptic bumper stickers and/or airline tags. Alone any one of them would look tacky, but taken together, they seemed to be wearing the fraternal jewelry of a secret lodge.

As they churned around, emitting waves of outrage, indignation and mystification, Malory caught sight of the words St. Germain on one of the buttons. This had to be the group Dave had come to meet. One neat little female in tight faded Levis was worth the trip across town just to look at. But Silver was nowhere to be seen, though Malory's other senses indicated he was nearby and getting nearer.

As one in a business suit approached, Malory listened.

"Listen up folks. The guy at the desk said they've never heard of any convention! They've got no room listing for Elrod. People have been asking all day, so they made up this flyer." A blonde wearing a T-shirt with Einstein's equations blazoned on the front and in back it had a picture of the galaxy with a YOU ARE HERE arrow, took the flyers and passed them around.

Meanwhile, the nearby elevator opened and more fraternal brothers and sisters poured out calling to the distressed group. One of the loudest voices was David Silver's.

"We've been had, guys, but it's okay. The Boca crowd decided to hold a con anyway. We've got a suite upstairs and a couple of local writers are coming. We've got a taper and a whole set of *Forever Knight*. Who needs crash space?"

The out-of-towners surged forward, and everyone was talking at once. A very tall, portly man carrying professional camera equipment, cut across the babble with a very, very loud voice. "When I find out who's responsible for this, I'm going to publish it in—"

"Chill out! We're making a fan legend here. This is better than SnowCon in New York back in the seventies!"

Just then the street doors opened wide and a crew of white-clad Red Cross workers jockeyed in two trollies stacked with equipment stenciled BLOOD MOBILE.

"You don't think—"

"I don't believe it—"

Someone started to laugh.

But Malory wasn't listening. A very familiar sensation was creeping over him. He scanned the vicinity for the source as the humid, rain-scented air swept through the air-conditioned lobby from the doors where the Red Cross crew wrestled with their equipment. Some posted signs.

Malory found the source of the sensation revealed by the mists of the fountain. Etched into the falling droplets was the dim suggestion of a face, the misty outline of a presence. Xlrud. His oldest foe.

Malory snapped his attention back to Dave who was leading the crowd toward the Red Cross workers. Even with every sense focused, Malory couldn't detect a hint of Xlrud's taint on David Silver. *I'm in time!*

Malory began to move, but the demon acted faster.

In the crack between seconds of Time, the demon coalesced as a human, and blended with the group's sense of continuity so all the humans perceived him as always having been with the Red Cross crew. Malory checked his mad dash to Silver's side. What was Xlrud up to?

The demon wore a white linen suit with a silk shirt and tie, looking every inch the tropical gentleman. He approached the group and gave a theatrical bow as if they had all come specifically to see him. "I am Phineas Norton Elrod," he announced proudly. "And as advertised, I will give a free Tarot reading to each and every blood donor who volunteers tonight." He bowed again. "I am so very glad you could all come." As he rose, he glanced up and caught Malory's eyes, flashing a mocking smile.

The demon was barely five feet from Dave and had the human's full attention. But it only lasted the barest instant, and during that time, the demon's attention was on Malory. *Dave's still safe.*

The crowd broke, whirled, and engulfed the Blood Mobile crew, helping them with their equipment, carrying the whole mob toward the function room set aside for the Blood Drive.

As they came past Malory's position, he heard comments on how the on-line BBS's spread distorted rumors as well as real news faster than the blink of an eye. Phineas Norton Elrod was indeed a P. N. Elrod, but not The P. N. Elrod, and he was certainly giving readings, but not of a new Vampire Files novel.

The laughter was rich and deep and equally as powerful as the outrage and indignation had been. These people were filled with the juice of life that Xlrud delighted in devouring. But his real prey was Dave.

Get Dave out of here and he'll leave those people alone.

Malory joined the churning mass of humanity, sensing the warm glow of vitality contrasting to the chill, silent hole around Xlrud. Moving with the current, he arrived at Dave's side just before they began to squeeze the equipment through the door. Malory touched Silver's elbow and murmured for Silver's ears only, "I have to talk to you."

Silver turned, started as he identified Malory, then glanced about with a frown. "Now? Can't it wait?"

"No. It can't. This is serious. Urgent."

Xlrud stood aside holding the door open for two Blood Mobile workers to dolly their equipment through, but he called to Dave, "I thought you were going to be first."

Silver looked from the demon to Malory and back, shrugged, and called to the crowd, "I'll be back in a while."

Taking Malory by the elbow, he wedged open a space and slid to the edge of the crowd. "Now, what's the problem?"

Xlrud's eyes bored cold shafts through Malory's back. "Not here. Outside."

As they moved away, the demon's silent laughter followed Malory. It was amazing what humans never noticed.

Rain washed air still heavy with Florida humidity greeted them when the doors opened. Silver stopped under the portico, away from a group hassling with luggage near the airport limo. "What's up?"

Malory edged closer and in a very private tone, said, "We've got big trouble. Very big." The chill of Xlrud's presence splashed through the plate glass and washed against Malory's senses. "Can we talk about it at home?"

Silver swept the now empty lobby with a glance,

and replied in a similarly private tone, "Hey, I wasn't going to donate blood—in case you need it. I just tell them I have allergies. I'd probably get the free Tarot reading anyway. Then Jeanne Kalogridis was going to read outtakes from the last book in her Dracula trilogy before we watched—"

"You can give blood to the Red Cross anytime you like," Malory interrupted. "Did you drive down?"

"No. I took the bus. Parking is ridiculous." He gestured at the rate sign.

The tailor couldn't get used to his new, more affluent, lifestyle. Malory reached out his arm to invite Dave inside his personal fields. "Then let me take you—"

Silver dodged back. "Come on, Mal. I don't want to leave yet, not unless it's really important. Some of these people are—"

"One of those people is a supernatural creature, and an enemy of mine, of a sort." To be honest, Xlrud had done Malory a favor or two upon rare occasions. "Dave, I told you I'd never ask this of you again, but...." He took a deep breath and plunged ahead. "I really need access to your mind. I have to be sure—"

"No!" But as he spoke, Silver took a step toward Malory, one hand out as if about to accept the mental intrusion. His voice rose an octave, and his lips snarled. Then he apologized. "It's not that I don't trust you, but Mal, you don't really want to! I mean—you promised!"

The last two words were a muted wail of anguish.

Malory sorted out two strong emotions from the melange assaulting his senses. Fear. Despair.

Very well. That's the end of the matter. The best he could do for Silver was to lead the demon away from him.

"And I will keep that promise. The lawyers will contact you in the morning. I'll make sure that you've been well provided for. Don't try to trace me. Remember your promises to me, and I will honor mine to you." He turned, then paused to offer, "My advice is to leave this hotel now, while you still can. I mean this very instant. There is nothing for you in there but disaster." He took two strides toward the deeper shadows, gathering his power.

"Mal! Don't go! Not without me. Please."

The vampire turned. "It's not by my choice."

"If it means that much to you—okay." He stepped closer. "I'll go home with you. We'll discuss it."

"Are you sure? This could become worse than it was in San Francisco. Much, much worse, especially from your point of view."

They were very close now, and Malory spoke softly, letting the rain and his power mask his voice. "There's a demon involved. I suppose that's what you'd call him. He works for my ancestral god. His missions are usually to destroy whatever I've come to treasure." Tentatively, Malory held his arm out. "In this case, that could be you. And I've never yet managed to thwart him completely."

David Silver willingly stepped into his grasp. "Maybe you're not a match for him by yourself—but with you and me together, he's the one who's got a problem, not you."

Since that awful escape from his burning house in San Francisco, Malory had practiced transporting Silver until the human was no longer so overcome with fear that he literally rooted them to the spot. But the vampire did have to take a superficial grip on Silver's consciousness, dimming his perceptions of the transition to mist. The process had become so routine with them that neither expected what happened.

The moment Malory turned through the alter-dimension to reformulate as mist, simultaneously damping Silver's awareness and mentally impelling them toward home in one operation, something grabbed him.

A hole irised open deep inside the kaleidoscopic montage that represented Silver's normal waking consciousness. Images flew into a vortex and Malory's awareness tumbled into the whirlpool of human thought.

But it wasn't human. Not entirely.

Xlrud. Everything was flavored dark and grimy like Xlrud's mind. But David Silver was there, too, sparkling with warmth and vitality.

In the still center of the blurred whirlpool, was a tiny image, sharp like a laser-enhanced photo, an aerial view of an ethereal city, a white granite building with gold doors surrounded by nested walled court yards. Among plentiful greenery, pastel-pink buildings lay interspersed with needle-like spires. The whole gorgeous city blanketed across a landscape of rolling hills. There were sharp little hummocks carved into terraces or decapitated and crowned with buildings, glittering buildings like scattered gems flowing across hill and valley alike. Taken as a whole, the place was a work of art.

The view descended to reveal detail, traffic and people.

NO! cried Silver silently and twisted in Malory's mental grasp.

The image shattered and the bits whirled away into fathomless blackness. Dizzy, disoriented, operating on the sheer momentum of intent, Malory reformulated their solid bodies inside their apartment living room.

The two of them tumbled into a heap of arms and legs, Malory fetching up against the sofa and Silver draped across the stacks of magazines on the coffee table. The slippery stack oozed sideways carrying Silver's limp body to the floor.

"No, Mal, no! Don't—"

Silver rolled to his side on the floor at Malory's feet, hands clutched to his head. "Stop! Don't! No!"

On Silver's temples, Malory now saw angry red welts in the shape of a hand, tapered, clawed fingers delicately placed just so. The welts enlarged as if the demon hands were enveloping the human's skull even as Malory watched.

I was too late! He was already in his mind!

And Xlrud had almost had Malory, too. But why? To what end?

Malory scrambled to his knees and pulled Silver into his lap. "Dave! Open your eyes! Look at me, Dave.

Dave!"

The human eyes opened, glittering with demon consciousness. "It's all right, Mal. Come into my mind!"

"Xlrud! Don't you—?"

"Oh, Mal, help me! He's got me!"

That was Silver.

Malory reached for Silver's demon-scorched face, and the human twisted away. "No! He'll get you too!"

The demon laughed with Silver's vocal chords and turned back to Malory, smiling seductively. Silver's hand shot up to encircle Malory's neck and pull him down.

Losing all physical awareness, Malory tumbled deep into Silver's mind. With that same dizzy, disoriented helplessness he'd had on arrival at the apartment, Malory fell into Xlrud's trap.

Had he never entered Silver's mind, never controlled that mortal body, he would not have fallen. Malory had opened the gateway inside Silver's mind himself. Xlrud only yanked him through it.

But as he spun out of control, he finally understood Silver's initial resistance to Malory's request. He'd been protecting Malory from the demon lodged within him, without even understanding what was happening.

Xlrud must have lured Silver to the hotel to plant that trap in his mind. But how? A demon had to be invited into a mind. Silver just wouldn't do that.

However it had happened, one thing was clear. Malory had to evict the demon without destroying

Silver.

Abruptly, Malory landed hard in the demon's illusion.

He was seated in a movie theater with a giant wrap around screen hidden by gorgeous red velvet drapes with gold fringe several feet high. *This has to be the nineteen-forties! Theaters don't even have curtains today.*

The sumptuous folds of draperies swept aside even as the projected images already danced upon them. But there was no screen behind the drapes. It was a huge window. Bright, daylight, blinding, searing white daylight, real daylight blasted through the window carrying daytime images that pierced his skull!

Ahhggg! Malory tried to jackknife forward to hide behind the seat in front of him, but his torso was caught in restraining straps. He felt his skin sizzling, the pain very, very real.

A voice that wasn't audible, Xlrud's voice rumbled, *Look upon the fate of Jerusalem and know what you see!*

Malory's burning eyes popped wide open, pricked as if held open by demon claws. His head jerked around. Hot demon thoughts forced his eyeballs into focus on the sun drenched city of Jerusalem—a Jerusalem of the far, far future.

Then Silver's face replaced the image of the city, filling the window that was not a theater screen. It was a homely face with a large nose, soft brown eyes, bushy black eyebrows, and neatly trimmed black hair.

The familiar face grew larger than the screen, and came hurtling toward them like the image of a train coming along a track. Just when the train would have begun to pass overhead, Silver's living body impacted on Malory's chest.

NO! Silver's scream filled the theater. Malory's chair toppled over backwards, suddenly detached from its anchoring bolts.

Malory found himself lying supine in the living room of their apartment before the toppled sofa, hurting, moaning, squirming away from pain.

On the floor by the upended coffee table, Silver writhed in silent agony, the seared imprints of demon fingers now separated by tiny strips of normal skin.

Malory pulled himself up. His skin felt as if he'd really been exposed to the noon sun. Appalled he thought, *I'd forgotten what sun can do.*

He forced his body to rise. The pain was incredible. When he was on his knees, he surveyed the scrabbling, whimpering human form on the carpet before him.

Sluggishly, he recognized the random movements as crawling. Though Silver's body made no progress, clearly he was trying to crawl to his bedroom. Malory's gaze fell on the bedroom door, the door he was unable to pass. Then his eye rose to the mezuzah.

He was in motion before he fully understood what he planned to do. And that, he realized, was what ultimately saved their lives. Even as his hand closed on the door jamb, Xlrud yanked his mind back to the sun-drenched theater. He lost awareness of his body, even as it moved.

Look upon the end of Time! commanded the demon.

It can't be real, protested Malory.

Oh, it is. Your little friend is a veritable gold mine of talent, prophecy being the least of them. It took nothing at all to open this window in his mind to look ahead through time. Look, my old foe, look and be free.

Abruptly, Malory understood. If Silver was a genuine precog, with the demon's enhancement this could be real, and if it were real, then once Malory had glimpsed the end result of The One's pact with Abram, he would be free of The One's decree that he must live to see it. He would be able to die. He would be free to die.

For the first time in all these millennia the possibility was real. The True Death he had often prayed for, begged for, could now be his through the auspices of David Silver, an insignificant son of Abram.

But Silver had become a tool of Xlrud. The God of Abram insisted on an exclusive contract. Silver would be left trapped between the two Potencies as Malory had been. Or worse. His soul would disperse. The True Death no mortal could ever face in the natural course of events.

Malory's outrage burgeoned into strength such as even a vampire could not normally tap. Dimly, without bodily awareness, Malory heard his own scream turn to a grunt of effort, followed by a splintering crack.

The sun's image beat out of the theater screen-window. He smelled his own flesh burning and knew

Death stalked him with real hope this time.

Surrender to death was beautifully seductive. Xlrud had given him his heart's desire, a way out of the trap of existence. "Why!" demanded Malory aloud. "Xlrud! Why now?"

"He's ready to accept your sacrifice, stubborn one."

Suddenly it was clear. The god of his fathers, ignored by mortals, had lost strength over the millennia. Now he needed the vitality the sacrifice of Malory's life would bring him, the sacrifice offered millennia ago, and refused.

But David Silver was not a willing sacrifice as Malory had been, and the City Malory's life had been offered up to protect had long since been destroyed. Even a god couldn't restore it.

Unable to see the doorpost ripped from Silver's bedroom door that he held in his hands, Malory thrust himself and the unaccountably massive burden toward where he'd left Silver.

He couldn't see Silver's physical form. But he felt the human warmth pulsing gently, and it drew him through the veil of his own throbbing pain.

The closer he came to the human, the less the scorching, blinding sun burned through his inner sight, and the less the massive burden weighed on him. He seemed to be going downhill. He heard his own rasping grunts turn to cries of immanent triumph.

Awareness of his physical surroundings growing, Malory tripped and sprawled over the warm lump of flesh that housed the human soul and spirit. In a hoarse whisper, all that was left of his voice after his raging screams, Malory pronounced the banishment, "Get thou gone, Oh, Southwind Spirit, and hound us no more!"

He couldn't bring himself to pronounce it in the name of That Which Is. If he had, perhaps that would have been the end of matters, forever.

All he could do was use his last strength to ram the post with its fully enabled magical ward flat against Silver's chest. The human's feebly scrabbling hands clutched it with greedy hunger.

At the moment of contact, Silver shouted, "Schema Israel! Hear, Oh, Israel—"

The rest was lost in a searing white flash that burned hotter than the vision of a future noon sun over Jerusalem.

That was all Malory remembered.

He came to with Silver dragging him toward the hidden door which now stood open in the mantle. The lethargy of dawn gripped him, though he was aware of the pervasive pain of raw solar exposure coupled to the throb of a deeper damage that some holy objects could inflict.

The human's face was reddened as if with sunburn, and he hissed and whimpered with pain as he pulled Malory's body along. "Mal! Come on, help me. You can do it. Just a little, and you'll be safe. Come on, man!"

With a mighty effort, Malory twitched a foot just enough for the heel to dig into the carpet and shove.

"That's it!" grunted the human. "Come on now, once more. Over the threshold!"

Malory pushed with his other heel, and suddenly they were within his chamber entry. The smooth flooring let his body slide faster, and then Silver dropped him on the inner chamber's floor and fell over his body, stretching out one arm to trigger the door closing mechanism, shutting out the pressure of light.

The next thing Malory knew he was waking into gathering twilight, the darkness of his chamber cut only by his dimmest lights. Malory lay on his bed, Silver slumped in his easy chair beside him. On the stand beside the chair, Silver had a cut-down kit, a doctor's field kit for inserting an I.V.

The moment Malory's breath wheezed into his lungs to protest Silver's obvious intention to give him blood, Silver jerked awake. He had already rolled up one sleeve. He placed the tourniquet with the ease of long practice. A moment later, he had the open end of a large syringe pushed against Malory's lips while with the other hand he set a timer.

When Malory jerked his head aside, Silver followed the motion, letting the blood flow. "You haven't healed visibly all night. You'll never make it out of here without help. Come on, Mal, you did this to yourself for me. Let me repay you. It's not like it's the first time."

And the blood was so sweet.

Soooo sweeettt.

It had never—ever—been like this. The balm flowed through him leaving warmth and curious relaxation in its wake.

He couldn't stop, not even when Silver placed a hand on his forehead and announced, "That's enough. Wake up, Mal."

He couldn't stop.

The human hand pushed gently, then more firmly. "Now. That's it. Stop now."

The hard tube slid from his lips, and reflexively Malory followed, lips parting in the vampire's snarl as he went for human flesh.

"No." It was a command, a simple, calm statement without a trace of fear in it.

With the luxurious blood flow broken, awareness swept through Malory. The rapture abated.

He stopped sucking, muscles locked against muscles, body half-curved in mid-air and shaking with the effort of holding back that primal strike. It would kill the human.

Silver had rejected Malory's offer of immortality. Malory had promised to respect that. *If I kill him, I can't bring him back.*

Malory threw himself to the far side of the bed, curling around the aching loss of the promised satisfaction, commanding the need for Silver's so sweet blood to abate. And to his intense surprise, it did abate.

It helped that Silver staunched the blood flow and wiped up every drop, neutralizing the scent with alcohol.

By the time Silver circled the bed to see if the thwarted vampire was still animate, Malory had almost recovered. "You shouldn't have done it. I told you not to."

"You look better already," commented the human. "But you've got to hunt tonight, even though it's early for you."

"I know." *But I can't. After that—experience— nothing less will ever be acceptable.*

Silver answered the unspoken thought, "It's not every night you defeat a demon from hell and nearly kill yourself using a mezuzah for a weapon, a weapon guaranteed to backfire in your face. You must be hurting in places you never knew you had. Things will normalize after you've done what you must. Pull yourself together now. You have to go. The night's wasting."

Silver kept on like that, quiet, supportive, encouraging, and not letting any of the distaste, no, the revulsion, he felt show in his words. Malory knew that Silver still cringed from the knowledge that a human being would die tonight to feed a vampire. But he pushed Malory through the mechanics of showering and dressing, then forced him to practice a few reformulations from human form to mist to bat and back until he regained a semblance of equilibrium. Satisfied, Silver ushered him to the window, promising that everything would be all right soon.

It wouldn't, and Malory knew that Silver knew that. Nothing would be the same between them again.

Opening the window, Malory paused, reluctant to leave the human unprotected. "Dave, I have to know something. It's important, or I wouldn't ask. How did

Xlrud get into your mind?"

"Exelrod?"

"Xlrud. The demon, the creature that almost killed us both. It can't get into a human mind without invitation."

"I don't know, Mal. I'd never invite a demon into my—the Ouija board! Naw—that couldn't...could it?"

"What Ouija board? When did you get a Ouija board?"

"I didn't. At the hotel. Someone had one. We were playing. It seemed to work. I mean really work. Could the demon have been working it?"

"That wouldn't be enough."

"We used an invocation. One of the dungeonmasters thought it would be fun."

Dungeonmaster? "Invocation? What invocation?"

"Awaken north wind and come thou south. It's Biblical poetry. How could that—"

"Xlrud's appellation is South Wind. He tricked you through your friends, but he didn't care about you or them. He was after me."

"He used me to get at you. I didn't know the mere memory of sunlight could hurt you."

Memory of future sunlight! "Not ordinarily. I'll explain it to you sometime." With the mystery cleared up, Malory felt better. "Just don't call the winds by their directional names, and you'll be safe while I'm gone." He reformulated and went to do what he had to do with as much clinical dispatch as he could muster.

At least he had already researched his next victim. He

hadn't the patience for research tonight, nor the confidence in his judgment that would leave his conscience as clean as it could ever be.

When it was over and the body of the drug runner's hit man, a superbly talented individual who would never have been caught by the law, had been thoroughly disposed of, Malory found a glimmering of optimism returning. His body had accepted the sordid, bitter blood even though his mind and memory found it inadequate by comparison.

His healing accelerated. By the time he returned to the apartment, his skin had stopped smarting and he could fly without wobbling.

But as he closed the window behind him and stood facing Silver who was kicked back in his recliner, Malory braced for the most devastating experience of his long existence. Silver's rejection.

He knew it had to come. It just had to. San Francisco had been nothing; a little ceremonial magick against vampire-hunting criminals. But this had been a direct encounter with an entity which could not exist within Silver's technologically derived world view. And Silver himself had started it all by answering a computer BBS posting, and playing a silly game with a mundane toy.

Silver's face was bruised, and he had plastered bandaids on his arms and hands. He wore an elastic support around his left ankle. The splinters of the door post had been vacuumed up, the furniture straightened. A bedspread covered the sofa concealing most of the torn upholstery.

Malory didn't remember how that had happened.

But the most remarkable difference in the apartment was the psychic silence. The mezuzah had evaporated. Perversely, Malory missed the noise. The place didn't feel like home without it. Only the furniture polish and after-shave marked it as Silver's residence...that and the packed suitcase sitting beside the front door.

Silver flicked his remote at the TV and the VCR display shifted to pause. He had been watching a tape, though he'd been staring at a series of commercials.

"Better?" asked Silver.

"Yes."

Silver got up to face Malory, and the vampire tensed. "I've been thinking, Mal."

"Good." *Damn.*

"Yeah. It took awhile for my mind to unglue. Maybe you can sort of take that kind of thing in stride, but I....Shit! I just don't think I can live in this apartment anymore."

"I fully understand. I'll see to it that all of our financial agreements are termin—"

Silver paled. "Am I fired for what I did to you? I know you said not to give you blood, but—"

"I thought you just said you're leaving."

"Not my job with you, just this apartment. Florida, too, if I can convince you to go that far."

"The Potencies can find us anywhere."

"So, then, why not go? Believe me, Mal, I know myself. I'll never sleep another wink in this place, and I—I just want to get away. Someplace with no weird associations."

"Anywhere you want, anywhere but the north pole. Half the year, the sun never sets."

"I was thinking more, say, New York? New Jersey? Connecticut?"

"Sure. No problem. Any particular reason?"

"Well, I saw this commercial about how to become a stock broker. I'd like to try that. If I could get registered and licensed and everything, it could save you a bundle in brokerage fees."

"Bit of a departure for you." The man had been a tailor for years, loved it and wanted to open his own shop before Malory had ruined his life.

"Yeah, I know it's strange. But I think I can do it."

It would provide the human with a good independent living if, no when, they had to part company. *It will happen. It will. Just maybe not too soon.* "Considering how you've been handling my finances, I think you can, too. I'll make you a gift of the course."

"You don't have to do that."

"I know." Malory moved to look at the television screen. "But I don't know why you're not leaving my employ and my presence."

"Why would I do that?"

"Because you don't like the company I keep among supernatural entities?"

"Didn't seem to me that one was your good-buddy."

"No. That one wasn't."

Unspoken words hung in the air between them. *You mean you're friends with some?* But the mortal wasn't ready to frame that question aloud. "Come on, Mal, sit down and watch *Forever Knight* with me."

"I've been meaning to ask you about that." The vampire settled on the torn sofa. The ripped upholstery reeked of demon, but the smell faded from his consciousness when the actor on the screen snarled and his eyes turned green. *Green?*

VAMPIRE'S FRIEND

David Silberman locked the door of his dry cleaning shop behind him. The sun was going down—not his favorite time of day anymore. But today, the eve of Yom Kippur, was the worst.

He moved out to the edge of the strip mall's parking lot and paused, staring down the side street toward the Orthodox shul and a way past that, his house.

There were still many cars in the lot of the strip mall and the street was full of traffic. The goyim didn't know there was anything special going on in the world of Magic.

David had never been very religious, not even by Reform standards, until he'd seen a Vampire invoke a pagan god's assistance—and get it.

He'd had another object lesson when that same Vampire had saved his life from a demon's attack by tearing down the doorpost of his bedroom and thrusting it into his arms, kosher Mezuzah against his heart.

He'd often wondered if the Mezuzah would have saved him if it hadn't been so perfectly kosher. But most of all, he wondered if he'd really been saved. In San Francisco, he'd participated in a revenge-murder, and now had a pagan serial killer for a friend. He'd gotten involved in idolatry, not just regular magic which would be bad enough. He'd never respected those who called themselves pious Jews but isolated themselves from other Jews and from everyone else. He'd just never had anything much to do with G-d. *So why is my conscience bothering me tonight?*

He just didn't want the supernatural in his life anymore. He wanted to forget the Vampire and just walk away from it all. But he couldn't. The mental Link was permanent, maybe Eternal. So he'd spent the last few months surfing the 'net for information, and every time had ended up at the website of this local shul reading something the Rabbi there had written.

As dusk gathered over the city, he felt the Vampire wakening in his mind, a growing buzz of not-quite awareness. The mental Link between them could only be closed, not vanquished. Lately, it made him feel... unfit.

He started down the side-street toward his house, walking on the side opposite the shul, still not sure what he would do. Before he'd left he shop, he'd emptied his pockets and put on shoes that had no leather in them. He wore a hat. He could go into the shul, even though he hadn't bought a ticket to the High Holy Day services. *I could just stand in the back.*

It had been a year since he'd separated from Malory Avnel, or Arnaud Lemieux as he called himself in New Jersey. All year, the Vampire had scrupulously avoided stirring the mental link between them. He owned and operated a Motel 6 on I-80, leaving David to his Fairlawn dry cleaning shop, studying for his stock trading certification and his spiritual nail chewing.

A morally upright, completely ethical, totally honorable Vampire who kills at least two humans a month calls me his friend.

Worse yet, I call him friend—most of the time.

He paused across from the shul. It had been a brick church, circa 1900 that had burned down. Only the foundation had been left when the Orthodox shul had bought the land.

Some people were arriving, parking their cars in the lot behind the shul where the vehicles would sit until after dark tomorrow. The women were dressed in various colors, many of them wearing white, the married ones with their heads covered. The men wore business suits, white yarmulkes, and kittels,—the belted white smock they would be buried in. There were no black hats and curls hanging beside their ears, but some men wore their prayer shawls while some carried theirs. The prayer shawls were white wool with black stripes. There wasn't a silk one; not a single blue striped one anywhere. Everyone wore sneakers and carried Machzorim—the prayer books that contained the day's special prayers. *I couldn't possibly fit in among them. I wouldn't know how to pray.*

"G'mar Chatima Tova. Come on, you'll miss Kol Nidre if you stand out here!"

David started, stifling a gasp. It was an older man with a fringe of white beard and a jolly paunch. A hand touched his elbow, urging him on across the street. "The Rabbi's drasha you can afford to miss, but not Kol Nidre when Yussel's davening."

"Yussel's davening?" He couldn't remember what davening meant.

The man held open the door for David urging him inside. "He doesn't just sing, he really prays, and the Gates of Heaven open."

Davening means praying.

They came to the inner door to the sanctuary on the men's side, a stream of men shuffling in before them. David hung back. "I don't have a seat."

"No problem. My son is home with his week old son and his wife. They're both sick, so you can have his seat. It's a mitzvah to miss shul, even on Yom Kippur, to care for the sick. We'll take turns staying home tomorrow, so you'll still have a seat all day. Manny Rubenstein," he announced, holding out his hand.

"David Silberman" he said giving the alias the vampire had created for him in New Jersey. He shook the firm, dry hand.

In a twinkling, the old man had procured a prayer shawl and machzor from a cabinet and installed David in the chair next to his own seat on the aisle near the door. While Manny exchanged greetings in Hebrew with the people around him, David arranged the shawl the same way everyone else had theirs. Then he looked at the black book in his hands.

The printing had worn off the binding. Inside, it had English on one side and Hebrew on the other. Finding the English index in the back, and discovering page 1 was at the end of the book, he turned to Kol Nidre.

So far his hands weren't burning—G-d wasn't rejecting him. He sat in a room full of ordinary people, facing three steps up to a stage with a beautiful cabinet, hung with a white drape. That, he had learned online, was the Aron Kodesh, no doubt full of Torah Scrolls.

An electric Eternal Flame hung over a lectern on the floor level facing the cabinet. On the stage, in front of the cabinet, another lectern faced the audience. Behind him a raised dais held the reader's lectern where men were gathering to begin the service. On the side wall a Memorial Plaque had a lamp lit beside every name inscribed on little gold plates. All pretty standard for a synagogue. But behind him, beyond a filigreed symbolic barrier sat the women and children, divided from the men. Everyone chatted as if this were just another ordinary day.

Then, a man opened the Aron Kodesh exposing the ornately dressed Torah Scrolls to view and everyone stood up, silence falling.

David stood. The silence became palpable. The silence tensed. The door in his mind beyond which the Vampire lurked slammed shut, leaking not a whisper of Malory Avnel's presence. *He's uncomfortable with the Torah.* The silence thickened. The silence thrummed.

A baritone voice inserted itself without disturbing the blanket of silence and proclaimed melodiously, "Kol" paused, and enunciated, "Nidre"—drawing the word out until it echoed back from the ends of Time—"Veesarey"—parting the fabric of reality—"Vshvuei"—sculpting the silence—"Vaharamei"—reaching to the beginnings of Time—"Vekonamei"—the Torah Scrolls glowed, as if floating beyond the Gates of Reality.

On the second of the three repetitions of the entire prayer, David lost track of the words, carried on the sound of the voice that dripped tears of dread sincerity and earnest entreaty. The man wasn't singing. He was representing the whole of the people of Israel before the Throne, as would the High Priest of the Temple.

On the third escalating repetition, David felt the Gates opening, felt the cold heat of Divine Attention, and somehow knew that attention was on him. A peculiar fear gripped him, a kind of painfully pleasant fear he'd never felt before during any of Malory's brushes with the supernatural.

Suddenly, he was standing in an ordinary room full of people, hiss of air conditioning dominating, lit with ordinary lighting. Then with an eruption of quiet shuffling and coughing everyone sat down, kids whining, and the sound of traffic passing outside with thumping stereos.

I don't belong here.

As the Rabbi rose to take the lectern on the stage facing the congregation, David put the prayer shawl and machzor on his seat, thanked the old man, and bolted for the door.

I am not going to try that again. I'll find a Reform synagogue if I ever feel the urge again. But I really, really don't want the supernatural in my life!

Outside, the street still bustled with Monday evening traffic. Three kids were playing basketball in a driveway. An airplane droned overhead. The sky was darkening, but you still couldn't quite see stars through the haze. No hint of the supernatural. No hint of time being visible, palpable, open to his senses from beginning to end.

Hands in his pockets, shoulders hunched, eyes on the sidewalk before him, he started toward home. He rounded a curve in the street, momentarily finding himself alone in the quiet residential neighborhood. Trees rustled, leaves crunched under his feet. A pigeon whirred to a stop, perching on a branch. It's dropping spattered audibly on the concrete beside his foot, missing his shoe.

Automatically, he looked up to Heaven, mouthing, "Thank You!"

Something streaked across the indigo sky leaving a rainbow froth behind, pointing to the space between two houses across the street. The rainbow froth evaporated without a trace, but David knew just where the something had come to rest—next to his own house.

No. It was a decision surfacing from somewhere below his belt and he knew he was going to investigate and get himself into the exact kind of trouble he wanted to avoid. *No.*

He crossed the street diagonally, cut across his own small lawn, and took the stairs to the porch two at a time. *No.* He fetched the key from the potted Holly, opened the door, and put the key back.

No. The neighborhood was unnaturally silent. The stars were visible. It was now truly Yom Kippur. And his shoes were clean of bird dropping.

He went in his front door, touched his fingers to the mezuzah and kissed them, closed the door, locked it, and went through the living room to the kitchen. His fingers where he'd touched the mezuzah tingled pleasantly. That had never happened before. *OK, You win.*

He went out the side door to look in the alley beside his house—the house Malory had paid for, in full, probably with money taken from the criminals he drank to death.

Buried in the thick ivy between the garbage can and the air conditioner was a lozenge shaped zone of scintillating color. *Force Fields. It's an Alien from Star Trek.*

He stepped back inside, closed the door and leaned against it.

The subliminal whisper in his mind that was the link to Malory was still silent. The Vampire wasn't giving him this hallucination.

Although a fan of science fiction, an avid viewer of all kinds of fantasy TV, David had considered he had a good grip on "reality" until he'd met Malory.

Star Trek is not real. Whatever is out there—is real.

He took a spare blanket from the linen closet and went back outside. In the full dark, the glowing bundle lit the alley. The people in the adjacent house were away at shul, though they'd left the lights on.

He crept around the garbage can and waded into the

ivy.

Nerving himself up to it, he touched the glowing bundle. His hand jumped back of its own accord and the colors flashed and swirled where he'd touched. But nothing else happened.

He threw the blanket over the colored light and rolled the limp, flexible thing into the blanket. It didn't seem very heavy, and wasn't even as long as he was tall. He heaved it into a fireman's carry and made for the back door. When part of the blanket touched the mezuzah, the light filtering through the blanket flashed white, then subsided leaving David's body tingling pleasantly, as his fingers had.

Whatever this is, it's not very evil.

It was heavier than he'd thought. By the time he reached the guest room, his knees were sagging. He dropped the bundle onto the double bed and unrolled it.

Seen against the dark blanket, the glowing oblong seemed to have some structure, three pairs of calyx-like segments folded up around it, meeting in a zigzag line down the center.

He wasn't about to pry the segments apart. It was either an alien from another planet sans starship, or it was supernatural. It had taken a good fall, and it was hurt. He knew what he had to do, but he thought about it very hard first. He really didn't want to.

He waited. He raised one hand to the ceiling and waved it suggestively, "Nu?" No response. *OK, you win.*

He picked up the phone, dialing from old habit—a habit unused for more than a year. The Vampire's answering machine said, "Leave a message."

"Malory? Pick up would you? This is David, and I've got a problem."

"Arnaud here. I doubt it's one I can help you with. I've been staying out of your way tonight."

The door in his mind trembled but stayed leak-proof. "Thank you. I do appreciate your effort. But I think you need to get over here. I've got something to show you—explaining just won't work."

"You're inviting me into your house?"

David heard the eyebrow rise to the never-receding hairline.

"Into my house, yes. Hurry."

The pause lengthened. "Half an hour. I'll bring the car."

"Fine, but hurry. Oh, and Mal, just in case it matters, please forgive me for any wrong I've done you this year. I sincerely apologize, and I'll do whatever it takes to make it up to you."

There was a long silence. "You are forgiven and you owe me nothing."

Forty minutes later, the Vampire rang the bell. Arnaud wore a dark silk suit with a conservative tie against a perfect burgundy shirt with a white collar. His shoes were polished to a fine gloss. He strode into the living room and headed straight for the guest bedroom without even glancing around. He had, after all, seen the place through David's eyes for a year.

The alien was still motionless on David's guest bed, wrapped in glowing swirls of color.

"Mal...."

"Arnaud," Malory corrected, absently as he circled the bed studying the oblong.

David told him everything, starting with the bird dropping that missed his shoe, the streak of color and working back to the otherworldly experience in the Orthodox Shul. "I'm not Orthodox. I never will be. I don't know why I went there."

"It wouldn't have mattered where you went. It would have happened to you anywhere. I told you, you can't hide from the Potencies." Malory reached out and touched the alien.

It flashed, and Malory's hand sizzled and jerked away. Suddenly there was a vaguely human-shaped image sitting up on the bed, shrouded in gossamer color, but definitely there.

Two amethyst eyes appeared in the head, though the features remained blurred as if by a veil, and two arms with proper joints and hands appeared. The zone of colored-shimmer unfolded and extended behind the being and the knees appeared, though the feet were shrouded in moving mists. The trunk of the body seemed androgynous, the skin a pearly white.

The eyes swept the room. The suggestion of a wide mouth, high cheekbones, aquiline nose, all in a pale face gave the impression of alarm, perhaps bewilderment—confusion not fear.

Rubbing his scorched fingers, Malory spoke. "I

know you?"

The being centered on Malory, assessed what he was, and scrambled back to plaster itself to the headboard. Before finishing the move, it relaxed, more of its face showing. "Oh, it's you!"

David blurted inanely, "You speak English! Ma.... Arnaud, does every demon in the universe know you?"

"Of course I speak English, how else could I deliver messages? Where's the demon, Meshobab?"

"There's a demon named Meshobab involved in this?" asked David, alarmed.

Malory said, "Sometimes they call me Meshobab. David, this Messenger is often called Bozez—or that's what some people call him because he shines so brightly. He's not a demon; he's one of the Messengers your God sends to Earth, usually with good news. Is your message for us?"

Bozez seemed to take a breath to answer, then froze, inspected the room, peered at David, and frowned. "I don't know. I can't remember." There was panic in Bozez's voice.

Malory was so stunned, he forgot to breathe.

David filled the sudden silence with the most inane remark he had ever uttered. "Well, you took a nasty fall. You'll remember soon."

Malory eyed David, and charitably ignored him as he deliberately took a breath to say, "Other than that, how do you feel?" He stood back, inviting the Messenger to stand.

Slowly the glowing layers of colored gossamer that

almost resembled a person hitched to the side of the big bed and stood.

Once unfolded, the being appeared to have wings extending behind it, and the glowing nimbus around it seemed to concentrate over its head.

David finally realized what he was looking at. The prophet Isaiah had described the Seraphim, and David had memorized the passage from a recorded reading by Theodore Bikel. "In the year that King Uzziah died, I saw the Lord sitting upon a throne, high and lifted up, and His train filled the temple.

"Above it stood the Seraphim: each one had six wings; with twain he covered his face, and with twain he covered his feet, and with twain he did fly.

"And one cried unto another, and said, Holy, holy, holy, is the Lord of hosts: the whole earth is full of His glory."

"You're a Seraph!" accused David.

"Oh, no nothing so glorious." Bozez fluttered nervously, but politely aware he was nearly filling the room, was careful not to knock the bedside lamp over. "I'm just a messenger." He looked worried. "But why am I here?"

Malory described the streak David had seen in the almost-night sky.

"I don't remember that."

"What is the last thing you do remember?" asked David.

"I was on my way down Jacob's Ladder." The being paced, wrapping his wings tightly about himself again.

He muttered in what sounded like several languages. Malory listened intently, and David watched Malory.

Finally, Bozez turned to Malory and said, "Either I slipped on something, or the Ladder broke under me just as the Gate opened. But I don't see how that could be.

"Is this Enemy action? Is that why you're here Meshobab?"

"I don't see how my god could be involved," answered Malory. "Even my god can't break the Ladder. But... cause you to slip? The demon Xlrud could do that, I think..."

Bozez considered that. "No, probably not without the Lord's help..." He whipped around to stare at David. "Where did you say you were at dusk?"

Mouth dry, David just stared. *I am not responsible for an Angel falling to Earth! No! I didn't do this!*

Malory repeated what David had told him of the experience during Kol Nidre.

David objected, "But the Gates don't keep Eastern Daylight Saving's Time. It's sundown at different moments in different parts of the world!"

Bozez heaved a sigh. There was no other way to describe the body-language message his not-quite body seemed to project. "I thought you had learned that from Xlrud. Time is a property of the Matter/ Energy Interface. It doesn't exist above the Material plane because—" He broke into a grin that spread from eyes and mouth to infuse his aura with a myriad bright, scintillating sparks until he was a blinding white.

Malory shaded his eyes and retreated toward the door. "I can't take much of that, you know, Bozez!" To David he added, "See why he's called Bozez?"

The Angel reined in his brilliance, folding in upon himself again.

"Sorry. But I remember!"

"Your mission?" asked David.

"No, just how Xlrud used you to try to get Meshobab away from The Lord and you foiled him beautifully." Deflated, he added, "But I've no idea what I was supposed to do here." The Angel sounded even more worried.

"My mother always said," started David. They turned to look at him politely. "Um, well, when you forget something, you should retrace your steps and you'll remember."

"Worth a try," allowed Malory. "Go on back up and see if you can find where you fell from. Maybe you'll remember. In any event, you can find out why you fell."

"I'm sure the Message had something to do with David and Time. You're probably right. I'll never remember as long as I'm embedded in Time. The Message may have something to do with why I fell. I'll be right back."

The gossamer wings of colored nothing unfolded and filled the room with shimmering blur. David was certain that the other two pair of wings also unfolded and whirred but he was too busy shuddering in awe to observe carefully. The whirring vibration produced by those wings apparently hit a note that resonated with the human nervous system.

Somewhere during this, he felt his body come apart into whirling sparkles, and coalesce again. And so did Bozez. Malory though, was no longer in the room.

"Did it work?" asked David.

"Would I be here if it did?"

"You said you'd be right back."

"Not that right-back. Meshobab! You can come back now." Bozez went to the door and opened it, moving out into the corridor.

"Meshobab? I didn't mean to get so bright, really I'm sorry to distress you…"

They found the vampire in the living room seated in David's reading chair, unsurprised at Bozez's failure to climb The Ladder.

"Something is wrong. The Gate is open. The Ladder is still there."

"Why can't you climb it?" asked David.

"I don't know. I can't get a grip. It's like there's a piece missing."

David said, "You're probably still stunned from the… impact of landing." *He is not a fallen Angel!* "It'll be better in the morning."

"I don't think so," said Malory. "That God of yours is up to something. Jacob's Ladder can't *break*. It *is* reality. His Messengers don't lose their memories. Xlrud might be playing some game here, but it wouldn't be working without Divine complicity. The Message is in this Situation somewhere. It's up to us to figure it out. And I think we only have until sundown tomorrow when the Gate closes."

That was the first sensible thing David had heard all evening. "I didn't mention," said David. They turned to him. "The old man—he said that missing the Service to care for the sick was a mitzvah. Do you think Bozez is sick?"

Malory considered the Angel. "No. He can't die."

"But he's in distress...he's lost, cut off."

"Scared," admitted Bozez with an air of shame. "Nothing like this has ever happened before, not that there is any such thing as before where I usually am."

"So our job is to get him back where he belongs," said David.

"And we have to do that before the Gate closes."

"How?" asked Bozez. "You can't climb."

"We could summon Xlrud...," started Malory.

"Oh, no!" objected David. "No way can we control that demon. Besides, summoning, trapping and forcing a demon to do our will doesn't seem like a very Yom Kippur thing to do."

"That's it!" Malory shot to his feet and began to pace. "We've been handed a problem and it's a test. We have to solve the problem within the rules."

"A game?" asked David, offended. "This is the most solemn holiday of the year!"

"A challenge. A lesson. A test," said Malory. "And it's not my god who's behind it this time. All this is beyond him. I can't even guess what this is really about."

David ran his fingers through his hair and shrugged.

"Me, neither." Other than what Malory had taught him, David knew nothing much about magic, and most of the fiction he imbibed wasn't very educational.

Bozez said, "I think David is right. I think I have to go back up to find out what it's about. And I can't."

"You need a boost," said David. "We need some kind of magic that can catapult you over the broken rung in the Ladder."

"The Ladder can't be broken," insisted Malory and Bozez in chorus.

"Well, the illusion of it being broken then. From our point of view, for us at this moment in Time, it is broken. Maybe everyone else out there praying up a storm is getting Messengers to bring them Enlightenment, but our Messenger has amnesia. It's up to us to help the Messenger, not the Messenger to help us. So what kind of magic can boost an Angel into Heaven?"

They exchanged blank looks. Malory, Master of so many Magical Systems he couldn't even count them all, just shook his head.

David paced the three steps across the living room and back again. He'd never paid attention in Sunday School. He'd memorized his bar mitzvah portion by rote, and actually had no idea what the words of the Torah actually said. All he knew about Judaism, he'd learned on the 'net over the last few months.

And suddenly he was back in the shul with Yussel's voice shaping the Silence into pure emotion, the image of the elaborately dressed Torah Scrolls floating in a haze of light, as if the inside of the Aron Kodesh was in another dimension. Over the Aron was inscribed the words sung in every Synagogue when the Torah was taken out to be read. Etz Haim, Hii.

"There's another way into Heaven!" said David. "There's Jacob's Ladder. And there's the Tree of Life. The Torah is the Tree of Life."

Bozez blinked skeptically.

Malory said, "They're really the same thing."

"But not exactly the same. A real Torah Scroll—not a printed book, but the real hand-written on lambskin, actual Torah—the actual words given to Moses—they have the power, the kind of Magic needed for this."

"I think he's got something," allowed Bozez cautiously. "It would be like climbing a different face of the Mountain. It's the same Mountain, but the terrain is different. There could be a glacier on one side while the other is clear. But we don't have a Torah Scroll. I can recite the whole thing from memory but memorized recitation doesn't penetrate to the Material plane the way the written document would."

"This night of all nights, every Torah Scroll in existence will be in use," said Malory. "The custom, as I recall—and I think it's still practiced — is for the men to learn Torah all night."

"I'll bet in Reform Temples they don't," said David, not actually sure.

"It wouldn't work unless the Scroll is perfect," offered Bozez.

"Magically perfect."

Malory said, "There's that shul just down the street

that David went to this evening."

"There'll surely be people there all night," said David. The kind of people in that congregation would surely observe such ancient custom—at least some of them would.

"Good," grinned Malory. "Then we won't have to break in."

David envisioned a Vampire, an Angel and a lapsed Jew breaking into an Orthodox shul in the depths of the night on Yom Kippur. Malory could pull it off. He could turn to mist and sift into any building, and he was an expert on alarms. *This is insane.* But David couldn't help grinning at the image in his mind.

"I can get us in," said Malory. "I can make anyone there think we're members of the congregation. The cabinet where they keep the Torah Scrolls is probably a decorated fireproof bank vault the way it is in most shuls these days. Tonight it'll be open so we don't have to crack the safe."

"I don't know their customs," warned David.

"I can blend in," said Bozez, "at least when I remember not to blaze up too brightly."

"If we blunder, I'll be sure no one notices," assured Malory.

"We'll just drift in, find a perfect Scroll, and Bozez will be on his way."

* * * * * * *

Five hours later, David was wondering how he could have thought it would be that simple.

The shul's front door had been unlocked, and they had just walked in ahead of Malory. But from there on it had gotten complicated.

Malory had winced and trembled at passing the mezuzah on the door, lagging behind them.

David had whispered to Bozez, "He's been telling me the truth, hasn't he? That he has eternal life because The Lord God of Abraham, the Creator of the Universe, Blessed him to offset the curse of a pagan god?"

Bozez regarded David meditatively. Then he allowed, "That's a good enough way to explain it. He's not Evil; he's just a victim. Don't blame the victim for the crimes of the victimizer. In fact, it's rarely a good idea to blame at all."

Behind them, Malory mastered his aversion and slid through the portal, hugging the left-hand doorpost, away from the mezuzah.

Then, in the lobby, he stopped, staring intently at the sanctuary.

Over a year ago, during their encounter with Xlrud, Malory had explained that his aversion to Judeo-Christian power was caused by his own god's curse clashing with the Blessing of the Eternal that he carried. The psychic noise did him no harm, but he suffered miserably—even debilitatingly. Now, he couldn't keep the effect from leaking through to David's mind.

"There are six men in the building," Malory reported from his Vampire senses. "Four in there, and two upstairs. I think six—no seven Torah Scrolls. Four in there, and the rest are upstairs."

One man emerged from the main Sanctuary on his way to the Men's Room and greeted them casually. "Nachman is learning upstairs, and the Rabbi is down here. I'll be right back."

They decided to join the Rabbi in the Sanctuary. A space had been cleared among the chairs and a long table had been set up. The table was covered in large, leather bound books, gold lettering on the covers, some open, some stacked.

As they came in, the Rabbi and a group of men were on the stage next to the Aron Kodesh, which stood wide open. The Rabbi, a young, energetic, clean-shaven man in shirtsleeves, was holding forth. Every once in a while David recognized an English word.

All the Torah Scrolls in the Aron had been moved to one side, and the back wall of the Aron was open. The light in the Aron dimly illuminated a large space beyond the back wall, almost another room, lined with shelves, stacked with books. There was even a Torah Scroll.

"So," concluded the Rabbi, "we'll have to get that latch repaired after Yom Tov. Meanwhile, be very careful not to lean a Scroll against the back of the Aron, it shouldn't fall open during davening.

"Chaim, remember not to let the time-lock engage after Ma'ariv tomorrow, and I'll have Irv get at it before Shacharis."

They carefully closed the back wall and rearranged the Scrolls so they rested against the side walls of the Aron. The one in the center was propped on a stand so it didn't lean against the back wall, and they closed the Aron, pulling the curtain across the door.

Then the Rabbi turned, saw them and greeted them heartily, inviting them to sit with him at the table. Everyone made room for them. David had no idea what they saw, he just grinned and nodded affably and pretended he knew what he was doing. The Rabbi began lecturing again in a mixture of languages.

Malory said, in a normal tone, "They will see and hear only three members of the congregation sitting here and listening intently even if we move about. And I was right, they didn't lock the Aron Kodesh, just closed it. Bozez, come see if you can find a Scroll that will work."

"Wait—he's missing the point..."

"Bozez, you're not going to sit here and teach the Rabbi are you?" asked David, unsure why he was appalled at the idea.

"Well, but The Rambam...no, I guess that wouldn't be a good idea until I find out what my mission is." He rose to go with Malory.

"M-Arnaud, wouldn't it have been easier to make us invisible?"

"Not in here with all this noise," answered Malory. "It's too hard to concentrate." Scrolls and even the books produced a discordant, psychic shrieking David could feel despite Malory's efforts to shield him.

"David, sit there and pretend we're beside you to keep my illusion going. Give us time to see if there's a Scroll here we can use."

Malory and Bozez went to the Aron and opened it. No one noticed. The Angel reached out to touch the Scrolls, and the whole Aron burst into a superheated blaze of white that surrounded Malory and Bozez and started to billow out to fill the room. Nobody at the table noticed. They were involved in an argument ever louder and more intense. It was vehemence more than anger, but it was a real fight.

It had seemed like an eternity before the two closed the Aron and came back to the table, defeated. Malory collapsed into his chair, and if David hadn't known better, he'd have said the Vampire was sweating.

Bozez said, "They're all very good, but none of them is perfect."

"We'll have to try upstairs, then. David, do you know where the stairs are?"

"I saw a broad, carpeted stairway in the lobby."

"Good." He paused, glaring hard at the men around the table.

"Now they won't remember we were ever here. Let's go."

Following signs, they found the upstairs hall, a large room normally partitioned for children's classes and opened for larger celebrations. For the High Holy Days, it was rigged out as a second shul with portable lecterns and a small, beautifully draped, Aron Kodesh on a small stage.

At the door, Malory stopped them. "It's not so bad up here. I think I can get these men to join the ones downstairs. Just a moment."

By the time he'd finished, and the two men had passed them on their way to join the Rabbi, the Vampire was shaking with the effort. *This is worse for him than he's letting on.*

But now they had the large auditorium to themselves. And their luck held. The less ornate, plain wood Aron wasn't locked. And one of the Scrolls was perfect—or perfect enough to suit Bozez. He blazed up so brilliantly that Malory complained again, retreating, and Bozez apologized profusely.

They took the jangling silver crown off the top spokes of the Torah's roller bars, pulled the long cover up, unfastened and unwrapped the binding strap, and put the scroll on the Reader's Desk to unroll it. "There, now see if you can use the words to Ascend," said David, casting his gaze upward and sending a fervent entreaty to Heaven.

Bozez passed his hand over the words, glancing apologetically at Malory, and then unfurled all his wings and filled the room with light, motion and color. But after a few moments, he shrank and wrapped himself up again. "Almost, but I can't get into it to climb—if that makes any sense."

"I have an idea," said Malory. "You're going to need to traverse the entire Scroll, from the Beginning Word to the very End. It's the whole thing—holistically— that is The Tree. The little excerpt you're looking at now is only a twig—it won't hold your weight." He began to move chairs. "Here, let's make a clear space to unroll the whole thing."

David looked at the diagonal length of the room, then at the Scroll. "It'll never fit."

"Well, let's see if enough of it will. Maybe it's like a plane runway. If he can get going, he'll take off before reaching the end."

They created an open strip of carpet from corner to corner of the room, carefully picking up bits of detritus, children's toys, and what-not to make a clean strip for the Torah. The Vampire's waning strength was apparent in his every move. He was in a hurry to get this done, knowing his strength wouldn't hold out against the forces in this building.

Bozez strove to keep his dazzling light down to levels Malory could stand, but as each page of the Torah Scroll was revealed, he got brighter and brighter. Finally, they had most of the Scroll exposed, laid out diagonally across the room. At last, Malory said, "OK, try it now."

Reverent, enraptured, and humbled, the Angel stepped out over the first words of the Torah Scroll, wings unfurling to fill the room again. *Here we have all these elaborate rituals for reverently handling a Scroll* thought David, *and he goes and walks on it!*

Bozez took a step, and then all David saw was a gossamer rainbow streak flashing along the length of the Scroll, and then his eyes just gave out from the brilliance.

When it was gone, the fluorescent lighting in the room seemed like total darkness.

He blinked his way back to Reality and yelled, "We

did it! MArnaud, we did it!"

There was no answer.

"Mal?" He looked around. The Vampire wasn't in the room. He looked behind the stacks of chairs they'd made, behind the lecterns, and then saw the door was slightly ajar.

He found Malory in the hallway, fallen face down, as if he'd been fleeing the room when he passed out. Kneeling beside the Vampire, David found him as dead as his daytime coma ever made him. He hadn't turned to ash, which was a good sign. But it was still a long time until morning. He shouldn't be in his coma yet.

David wasted several minutes poking and prodding, pleading with Malory to wake up. He even tried opening the door inside his mind to let Malory talk to him mentally, as he had sometimes done during the day. Nothing.

Without Malory to control what the men were seeing, how could he get them out of the building? They'd walked down the street from the house, but David knew he'd never be able to carry the Vampire home, even if the street was wholly deserted which it wasn't.

He thought about going to get his car, but where could he hide the Vampire while he was gone? And there was the mess they'd made of this room. If people found it like that, they'd have the police here looking for a vandal.

And it would be daylight soon. He couldn't take Malory out in the sunlight.

He dragged the limp body back into the room and set about rolling up the Torah Scroll—normally a two-man job. He knew he'd never get it set to the correct page—he couldn't read a word of it—and he didn't even try to get it rolled up snug and tight enough. It was a big struggle to get the binding wrapped around it and fastened, and then with nobody to hold it upright, it was hard to get the covering in place because the spokes weren't close enough together and the Crown and Pointer wouldn't fit right either.

He'd just have to leave it that way, hoping they'd think some children had messed with it.

Rearranging the furniture by himself took more than three times as long as it had taken the three of them to move everything.

He could barely budge the lectern by himself, and the rows of chairs had to be set up straight.

All that while, Malory lay dead, not breathing, heart not beating. David worked against the clock, but still by the time the room was presentable, it was close to dawn. He couldn't get Malory out of the building now before people began arriving.

And he had to get Malory out of sight and store him where no sunlight—or children, would get at him until nightfall. Soon the building would be full of bored children and even more bored babysitting teens.

Usually, when badly hurt, the Vampire would recover with sunset. Maybe not this time, though. *Then what will I do?*

He opened the door to the hallway and peered out.

Voices rose from the lobby—the small group of men who had learned all night discussing going home to freshen up before the day's services. "No, we shouldn't lock up. Tully will be here in a few minutes." A toilet flushed. A door opened, and the voices faded. The door closed, echoing through the empty building.

A few minutes. How long is that?

He had one chance, and he knew Malory would never thank him for saving his life this way. But the one dark place the children would not go was the cabinet behind the Aron Kodesh where they stored the books that were so damaged they couldn't be used anymore. The psychic "noise" that so disturbed the Vampire would be greatest there. He'd have daymares from it. It wouldn't actually harm him, but it would make him helpless.

He's just stunned from Bozez's light. He'll recover, and everything will be fine. If we can get away with this, he...and I...won't have to move again.

The Vampire was much taller than David. In one corner of the room, there was a dolly used to move the folding chairs. How he'd get it down the stairs, David had no idea.

How had they gotten it up here? Where were the chairs normally stored?

He unloaded the rest of the chairs from the dolly, pulled and heaved the limp body onto it, and jockeyed it out the doors. The dolly about filled the hallway, and it was too wide for the stairs. He raced up and down the hall, past school rooms, and finally found an elevator in a corner.

As he reached for the button to summon it, the doors opened. He propped them open with his tush as he sidled the dolly into it. He ended up on the wrong side from the control buttons, and as he was maneuvering over the dolly to reach them, the doors closed and the elevator descended to the only other floor in the building. Then he remembered. The Orthodox wouldn't push elevator buttons on the Sabbath or Holidays, so they had the elevator rigged to run automatically all day.

It opened at the back of the caterer's kitchen right across from a huge closet full of folding chairs and what looked like a collapsed party-tent. He was tempted to store the body there. But the doors were open. Someone might want more chairs, and then what?

Maybe rolled in the tent? But it was trussed up neatly, and no doubt was huge and heavy. And he didn't have much time.

He made for the Sanctuary, battering the swinging doors open with the bumper on the front of the dolly because he couldn't stop it in time. The dolly wouldn't go more than a yard into the room, there were so many chairs in the way.

Racing the clock, he ran up to the Aron, pulled the curtain, opened the doors—lofted a hearty prayer of thanks that the doors were unlocked,—carefully and reverently moved the central Torah Scroll, pushed open the broken door in the back, ran back to heave and drag the comatose Vampire up onto the stage, pushed the flopping body through into the dark cubby, where it fell in an awkward pile, replaced everything, closed up, and ran back to the dolly which was propping the door open.

"Oh, you didn't have to do that! It is my job, after all."

Aware of beads of sweat rolling down face and body, David looked up to see a wiry old man in black with fringes hanging out from under his jacket and a very large white yarmulka on his head smiling at him.

The shock paralyzed David.

"Here, let's get this back upstairs," offered the old man, pulling the dolly out of the doorway.

David went with it. "Uh, um, well, I didn't finish in there yet. I thought I'd be done before you got here."

"That's very nice of you—uh—I don't recall your name."

"David Silberman. I own Silberman's Drycleaning. I'm not a member here, but...."

"You wanted to do a special mitzvah for us. Our gratitude will be with you."

The old man insisted on helping replace the dolly, then pulled David into continuing his routine of picking up and straightening the covers on the lecterns, checking and arranging, returning books to their proper places, sorting the chairs according to the names on them by the chart on the wall, all the while reciting the rules about what they could and could not do on Yom Kippur to make the shul ready for the crowd. He wouldn't even knock down a cobweb.

All David could think of was the Vampire behind the Aron Kodesh. Malory's subliminal pain leaked through the portal in David's mind and he was beginning to regret this decision. There were nearly fourteen hours of this to endure. Even if he went home, he'd still feel Malory's anguish.

But he couldn't go home. He had to watch. He couldn't leave Malory alone here, rendered helpless by daylight and the excruciating psychic noise. But, if that rear door fell open, what could he do to prevent anyone from discovering the Vampire?

I should have hidden him in the shrubs and gone to get my car.

No, I'd never have made it.

Heaving a dead body out of the shrubbery in front of a shul at the crack of dawn on a weekday on a busy street—no. On Holidays, the police patrolled the synagogues with special attention, particularly at night. He knew he'd have been caught. Irrational as it was, he knew it.

Eventually, the old man noticed him stopping to stare at the Aron Kodesh. "It is beautiful isn't it? It was made by one of our members, an artist. The Sisterhood made the drape for us, every stitch by hand. Wouldn't think anyone did hand embroidery these days, would you?"

"Uh, not like that. It's magnificent." It really was, but that wasn't the focus of David's attention at the moment.

"Young man like you...not married, are you? Ah,

didn't think so, well, I'll talk to my wife about that after Yontef. People will be here in a few minutes. Let's check upstairs."

OK so it's not so different from a Reform Temple. The main business is always getting everyone married off.

They climbed the stairs together, David aching in every joint, moving as slowly as the old man. He pushed into the upstairs auditorium ahead of David and stopped. "Did you do this?"

"Uh, no," lied David. "Is something wrong?"

"No, it's just that the chairs are all straight. Let's get the table put away and check the Seforim."

They folded up and stored the table, stacked the extra chairs, and collected the stray books, putting them back in the shelves.

While they worked, people began to sift into the room, the noise from downstairs growing every time the door swung open.

As they went back down, the old man offered him another seat he knew would be vacant, but David explained he'd already been invited by Manny Rubenstein to share his son's seat.

"That's just like Manny. Terrible thing about his grandson. If you need anything, just let me know. I'll see you after Neela."

Neela?

Then Manny arrived and collected David as if he belonged to his family, settling him with all the books he'd need. "Missed you for Ma'ariv last night. Glad to see you this morning. Yussel will be davening Musaf."

"That's wonderful," agreed David clueless.

There ensued five hours of ever growing, frustrated bewilderment. He never stood, sat, bowed, pounded his chest, or sang out an Amen on cue. Every so often, Manny or his son who replaced him periodically, would peer at the prayer book David held and flip some of his pages backward or forward for him, then point to the Hebrew text. After a while, they gave up and just swapped books with him, giving him the correct page.

The congregation sang four-part harmony as if they'd rehearsed for weeks, but most of the time only the men's voices could be heard. There were long songs, responsive readings, and at odd moments, while the Reader was chanting, the congregation would burst into song for a sentence or two, then fall silent. And all of it in Hebrew. There was no way to follow it in English, but everything seemed to be repeated and repeated again.

After an hour or so he gave up and just watched the clock, trying not to concentrate on the growing headache from Malory's pain. And he prayed. *Let Malory—Meshobab—recover! And let us get away with this. Just think how upset everyone here would be to discover a Vampire in the Aron Kodesh on Yom Kippur. We can't have that, can we? And I'd really like to know why Bozez fell off The Ladder, and if he's all right now. Ok, it's idle curiosity. I don't really need to know, but I'd like to. I took a liking to that Angel.*

And he kept arguing as best he could while the congregation prayed unintelligibly.

At breakfast time, he got hungry but when his stomach realized it wasn't going to get fed, it shut down until lunch.

The Rabbi spoke for about half an hour and David almost understood his point. "The Hebrew word for "sin" is "Chet." The prayer "Al Chet" is a comprehensive list of sins for which we ask Gd's forgiveness. The word "Chet" also means to "miss." When one misses a target, this too is "Chet." Teshuva—repentance—is not only for sins which one may have committed, it also encompasses failure to fulfill whatever potential G-d gave us. That too is called "Chet" and requires amending our ways."

There was a lot of his potential he hadn't lived up to. He'd been taking the coward's way out for the last year, just because he was uncomfortable with having Malory in his mind, and Malory's supernatural friends—and enemies—in his life.

Right after the Rabbi's talk, Yussel took the podium and once more, for David, the Gates opened.

As the feeling of G-d's attention on him intensified, the pain from Malory's distress receded. He even forgot to be embarrassed when everyone around him dropped to their knees and put their foreheads on paper towels they had spread on the floor. They did it several times, and the final time he actually managed to go with them.

While he was curled on the floor, with Yussel crying out a Blessing in tones of raw entreaty, David suddenly knew he was guilty, and G-d loved him anyway. Tears erupted from somewhere deep within and wracked him with sobs.

As they stood up and rearranged their prayer shawls, people passed tissue boxes around and many noses needed blowing.

It was after two p.m., right after the men of Cohen ancestry had trooped up onto the stage in front of the Aron to recite the Priestly blessing when Bozez appeared again.

It was the first time all day that Malory's hiding place was out of David's sight behind a wall of bodies, and it made him nervous. If that broken door in the back wall of the Aron should fall open, the dormant body would be discovered and mistaken for dead. The sun was streaming into the windows, lighting the whole area. The vampire might combust.

The Cohenim hitched their prayer shawls up over their heads while facing the Aron. The Reader called, "Cohenim!" and they turned to face the congregation, arms raised under their shawls, hands spread but invisible to the people. Most of the men around him had raised their prayer shawls or buried their eyes behind their books, or turned their backs. But David didn't copy them. He couldn't take his eyes off the Aron with so many people up there.

As the Cohenim repeated the words the Reader sang, in slow, solemn, precise tones, drawing out each word with melodic chanting in between, David felt a strange warmth and saw light swirling and gathering around and above the group of men. In the midst of the brightness, the compact form of Bozez appeared, glowing in shades of white, and unfolding rainbow wings until David could see his face well enough to recognize him.

The Angel's voice rose out of the men's chorus, blending the voices into a supernal harmony. The sound resonated in David's bone marrow, turning his flesh to gossamer light.

As the final word, Shalom, Peace, filled the room, Bozez swept his wings around himself, turned toward the Aron and held his hands up in the position of the Priestly Blessing. David knew it was for Malory. Then the overly bright Angel glowing even more intensely, flicked out of sight. A moment later, he was back. He looked David right in the eye, and formed words in his mind. "Oh, my Message before was that you should learn to enjoy the humor of the Situation. It'll make life around Meshobab much easier. Thanks for the lift!" A flash, and he was gone again.

The Cohenim shuffled and rearranged themselves completely oblivious to the Messenger, then the congregation was singing again. A number of people were wiping their eyes with tissues, but nobody had noticed the Angel.

They took a break then, many people going home for the interval, but the Rabbi gathering a group to learn more about the customs of Yom Kippur. David didn't dare leave except for a few moments to go to the Men's Room.

And an hour or so later, everyone came back again for the afternoon service. It seemed to David that they did everything all over again.

The next time they repeated "Al Chet" it turned him inside out.

He could think of an instance where he'd committed each and every sin listed and somehow he understood what he had done wrong, and why it was wrong. He was truly horrified at his own stupidity, and he deeply regretted every instance. He couldn't make amends if he lived a hundred lifetimes.

Then he remembered what Bozez had said about Time, about Malory being immortal, about what it would be like to look at human life from an immortal perspective.

We take our sins too seriously—that's why we keep doing the same thing over and over. We don't deal with the current Situation.

We react to memories of similar Situations in the past and fail to live in the present—and we miss the point. It's not that we take ourselves too seriously, it's that by reacting to new Situations as if they were in fact the old Situations that they resemble, we fail to live up to our potential. My current Situation is that I have the Supernatural in my life. I can't get rid of the Vampire without getting rid of G-d.

While he was still dwelling on how stunned he was by this revelation, and how much simpler it would make his life if he could manage to remember that insight after all this was over, someone blew the shofar.

It wasn't a recording, and it wasn't a pipe organ faking it. It was an actual, real, once-part-of-a-living-animal ram's horn someone blew their own breath into. He'd never heard anything like it before.

It was a soul-shattering sound.

Each individual peal vibrated all the way through his flesh, sizzled through his brain, turned his eyes to jelly, and made him need to scream with fear, ecstasy, elation and humility all at once.

When the sound stopped, the Gate was closed. He knew it, all the way through to the center of beingness. He was no longer a focus of Divine Attention.

And with that, Malory's distress grabbed his whole mind and heart.

But a new Reader took a place at lectern near him and everyone kept right on praying. According to the prayer book, they were doing the Evening Service. It was several pages long, but they raced through it all at blinding speed which was just as well since Malory was awake and hurting worse than ever. The Vampire was helpless and scared, and just short of panic.

Hang on, Mal, I'm coming to get you out of there. It'll be all right. Bozez came back.

He felt the vampire's pained astonishment at his use of the Link. He was weak, and confused, but replied, "Take your time."

And then people were leaving. David had to thank the Rubensteins, and give his phone number to the old man who wanted to find him a wife.

The social amenities were very brief since it was a mitzvah not to delay breaking fast. And David managed to contrive to hide himself behind the open door of the book cabinet in the sanctuary as the old man was closing up. Shortly, the building fell into utter silence except for the cars starting outside, and people calling happy greetings.

When he was certain everyone was gone, he came out of hiding.

All the lights were off except for the Eternal Flame, which could hardly be called a light.

By feel, he groped and stumbled his way up to the Aron. As he had guessed, the time-lock was not engaged, as the Rabbi had instructed, which meant that someone would be along soon to fix the latch. He turned on the little light inside the Aron, moved the Scroll and opened the back panel.

He found the Vampire sitting Indian fashion among the worn out books, the old Torah Scroll cradled in his arms, his head tucked down because of a low shelf, suit rumpled, tie askew, wearing a pained expression. "Dare I ask what happened?"

An Angel took a pratfall to teach me to have a sense of humor!

Something inside David gave way and he burst into divinely inspired laughter.

THROUGH THE
MOON GATE

Remora made camp in the high pass overlooking the Waste. She was still far above the sudden, frightening flatness that spread northward before her as far as she could see.

Off to her left, the sun was setting, a huge glowing coal kissing the horizon. It would be hot tomorrow, absolutely the wrong time to be crossing the Waste.

But what choice did she have? She forced herself to look down into the bleak, broken country. She had been born and raised in the Dales, surrounded by tree-shrouded mountains. She found her heart pounding at the thought of walking out onto that sere plane. It wasn't safe.

A thought trembled to the surface: *I'll go back.* Her clan tended herds, grazing them in the high valleys. *No, I won't go back to chasing smelly cattle around the mountain peaks!* She would not go back to being laughed at when she dared to mention her visions of the Old Ones.

She was short, stocky, and not at all pretty. Her face was weathered to a dark tan. Her hands were callused, and her legs lumpy with muscle. People looked at her and saw a worthless orphan, a drudge of doubtful parentage. Not even the wise woman considered her visions real.

"You put yourself above your station, Remora!" they'd say. "Now haul that bucket of slop, and stop this nonsense."

No, she was not going back. She'd find Arvon and the Old Ones or die trying.

With that settled she gathered firewood, and skinned the birds she'd brought down with her sling. In the days she'd been working her way through the passes which had been known to her only in nebulous tales, she had gradually learned to set a secure and comfortable camp. But she bore the scars from several nearly fatal errors.

Thus, she built a large fire, and sat up late watching for hunting creatures. They said four-footed beasts roamed the edge of the Waste in packs. But this night, all was peaceful. Light from a large, full moon came flooding over the peaks around her, and she rose to stretch and answer the call of nature before rolling up in her blanket.

Moving off to her left, she rounded a large outcropping and tended to her needs. She was arranging her clothing when she noticed the soft chuckle of water over rocks. Her water skins were getting low, so she followed the sound thinking of the bright taste of fresh water.

Through a narrow cleft, she found where a thin

stream dove down a crevice. Climbing a bit, she peeked over a boulder expecting to see the stream emerge. A watering hole would make good dawn hunting. But what she found set her gripping the sharp edges of stone under her hands until they hurt.

There, in a cup surrounded by steep, shrub-covered walls, was a place of the Old Ones.

A soft green carpet covered the ground. Huge undressed stones had once stood sentinel in a circle, but now most had fallen. Several stones still supported top pieces. It seemed like a building, but one that only defined an area rather than cutting it off from the elements. In the center of the stones lay a perfectly circular pool of water, glowing whitely under the fullness of the moon.

It seemed as if the few remaining stones somehow focused the whiteness into the water, and Power gathered there.

She took a deep breath, only now realizing she had stopped breathing. Without actually deciding, she found herself edging over the lip of the cup. The pale light shimmered in sheets between the stones, forming a protective wall more formidable than any keep's stone battlements.

She circled, cautiously, resisting a silent call. On the far side, she came abreast of three standing stones forming a door. On the right pillar a glowing area pulsed strangely. Around its edge, runes marched in a circle. She couldn't read them, but something reached out to her murmuring a promise, pulling her heart to safety.

Just then, a night hunter cried on the peaks above, and Remora started violently, stumbled, and was inside the circle. Peace engulfed her. She padded over to the edge of the pool and knelt, searching her mind for a prayer. There weren't many. She had been excluded from any talk of moon magic, and she had never related to Gunnora who was worshipped by so many wives. Those Who Set the Flame didn't sound very wise to her.

In any event, this place was older than any of those. She placed her palms on the surface of the water, hardly surprised to find it warm and coated with a soft mist that refused to let her submerge her hands. "Let the powers that blessed this place flow forth in abundance to bless the world in light. May I find acceptance in your eyes."

On one level, she was embarrassed by how childish she sounded. But tears flowed, and her breath came in gasps as she mourned for all the years she had been starved for this.

The moon sailed overhead, the light pouring through her body as if she were as insubstantial as the mist that gripped her hands. Power went through her, soft, silken power.

And then she saw it. Huge and black, in the bottom of the pool, it undulated until the whole pool heaved with it. The edges were curved into wicked points. Then, as it loomed larger, it turned up to her the white face of a man.

She screamed.

Remora had never been given to screaming, but what came out of her now was the screech of pure terror.

The pool surface broke open and spewed forth the demon. It shot into the air, and right before her eyes folded its blackness back across itself, and somehow, before it splashed down into the pool, it became a man in a black cloak.

Remora clamped her lips shut and swallowed a whimper.

No one grew up in the Dales without hearing of the Wereriders and all kinds of tales of Were-magic. Shapechanging. It happened. It wasn't, she told herself, necessarily evil. But her feet wanted to run.

The moonglow faded rapidly out of the pool as if bled off. She was aware of the shimmering walls spread between the stones going dark and winking out. She knelt beside an ordinary pond, under ordinary moonlight, and watched a man in a heavy black cape thrashing weakly.

Flinching away from the edge of the water, she stared fascinated as the man coughed, spat, and fought. It was almost funny, except that it finally hit her that he was truly helpless. She watched with a frown pinching her face as the figure curled into itself as if in mortal agony, and then, with a strangled cry, sank again beneath the surface.

He can't swim!

She peeled off her tunic, yanked off boots, and, not bothering with her heavy winter trousers, dove into the pool.

It was very deep, and very cold. She hadn't expected the shock. A moment before the pool had been blood warm.

She managed not to gasp, and when she forced her eyes open, she discovered that the water was so crystal clear that the moonlight penetrated nearly to the bottom. She spotted first the unnatural white face and hands and kicking, she scooped the unconscious form into her arms.

Her well-muscled legs thrust them to the surface, and she towed her limp burden by his sodden cloak to the rim. By the time she'd jackknifed the limp figure over the lip of the pool, she was wondering why she'd done such a foolish thing.

Before she could even consider throwing him back, he was coughing and sputtering. She crawled out of the water and heaved the now struggling man onto the greensward. "Take it easy, stranger. You breathed some water, that's all."

"That's all!" he managed. "To my kind, water can be deadly!"

"Then what in the Name of The Lady were you doing in there!" She was bending to wring out her trouser legs when it hit her that she'd understood him as if he were speaking her own dialect. But he was certainly no Dalesman.

He sat up, knees bent to prop his elbows. Regarding her with the same gaze she'd expect from a lord passing through her village, he challenged, "I might tell you if you'd tell me how I got in there!"

"I should tell you how you got in there!" She heard the furious indignation in her voice, and quailed, waiting for the lord to deliver one of those withering judgments that always came her way.

Instead, he cocked his head to one side, and asked, "You mean you don't know? You didn't do it?"

"Do what?" *Maybe I did.*

He looked about, and his face spoke clearly of inward bewilderment liberally laced with fear. He recited, half aloud, "I was flying along on my way to Denver. I had a midnight appointment with Irene. The snow pack was two feet deep. I was flying low because we were totally socked in. I remember—there was a Lear jet. I was knocked head over teakettle by the wash...then... Good God, this isn't Denver, is it?"

Remora hadn't followed all that, but the question was clear enough. "No, I don't think this could be Denver. I've never heard of any such place."

"Los Angeles? This is a movie set, right?"

She shrank away from his vehemence.

His lips worked, and his panic submerged as he reached out to her. "Look, don't be afraid. I don't—I won't hurt you. I thank you for saving my life. You must be chilled."

She watched his lips, then his eyes. A hard knot in her chest warmed and let go. "I believe you won't hurt me." *Stupid! I ought to run.*

A pack of hungry nightrunners yammered, voices echoing off the peaks. The stranger made a feeble attempt to wring out his cloak. She couldn't take her eyes off him. His skin was the color of moonlight, his eyes dark coals. His hair slicked back into a black cap, but it ended at the nape of his neck. His eyes met hers, and she felt his loneliness like a pain inside her.

"I have a campfire. Over there." She gestured with her chin. "We should get dried out." *Why did I say that?*

He followed her docilely. At the camp, she built up the fire and offered him a blanket while his clothes dried. "I don't own anything that would fit you."

"I don't suppose you would," he chuckled.

His voice soothed her in a way she'd never felt before. She tore herself away, and dragged out her spare clothes. When she'd changed, she returned to find him with the blanket twisted and folded about himself in a strange style, covering one shoulder and making a skirt about his waist. She wondered how he'd accomplished that, but silently bent to help him build a rack near the fire for their garments.

His were the strangest things she had ever seen. There were closures that just stuck together and made a tearing sound when parted. There were others that miraculously clung together and parted silently. And his cloak clasp displayed a huge red gem set around with clear ones that gathered the firelight. It must have been worth three fortunes.

She held it in the palm of her hand and asked, "Would you favor me with your name, lord?"

He cocked his head to one side. "I haven't been addressed that way in—" He seemed to catch himself.

"The lands where my father ruled are far away, and the country he ruled no longer exists. My current name is Dorian St. James, and you may call me Dorian."

The sadness throbbing through that speech almost made her want to cry, and in a fit of needing to comfort him, she replied, "If it is your wish to be called Dorian, lord, then I shall call you Dorian." She handed him back the clasp.

He took it and pinned it to the blanket, a wistful smile playing about his lips. With an effort, she asked, "Are you hungry?"

Taken aback, he answered, "How did you know?"

"I have some jerky here, and there's a little—"

"Ah! Your forgiveness. I shall not take your food. Such an act is not permitted to my kind. May I ask how long you expect it to be until the sun rises?"

"Oh, half the night is not yet gone."

His relief shocked her, but he distracted her by asking, "And your name? Would you favor me with such knowledge?"

In a rush of pleasure to be asked instead of commanded, she told him, "Remora. I served in Mistdale."

He bowed, putting his head down to the level of her waist. "Remora of Mistdale, I am at your service."

Her face went hot, and the tips of her ears burned. "Oh, no, I am nobody...."

"To me, you are She Who Saved My Life. Could you perhaps tell me how far it is to civilization?"

She waved back toward the south. "That way, about

ten or maybe fifteen days' travel, there's Eroffkeep."

He paced to the edge of the camp, where she had stood to look down at the Waste. As if the moonlight were enough to show him what she'd seen, he asked, "And down there?"

"The Waste. I'm going to cross it. But I've no idea how big it really is."

He turned. "Alone? You're going to cross that, alone?"

"Certainly, I'm going to cross it alone!" She turned her back and stirred the fire.

His chill hands closed over her shoulders and he turned her to face him. Looking down into her face, he breathed, "I meant no offense. Where I come from, even my kind would quail before such a barrier."

"I didn't quail from rescuing a demon from a pool of the Old Ones, did I?"

One elegant brow arched upward in Dorian's white face. "A demon? Is that what you thought? Then I owe you more than I ever knew." He tilted her chin up with one finger, and she felt the strength in him, strength that could crush her. But he held her gently as his voice caressed her. "And I have no right whatsoever to ask what I must ask of you. If I were the lord you thought me, or even the demon, I would offer to see you safely across the Waste. But I cannot do that, Remora."

His face lowered toward her, and his eyelids lowered in anticipated pleasure. She was sure he was going to kiss her on the neck, and she didn't know how she wanted to respond except that the thrill that warmed her prompted total surrender. *Idiocy!*

Her virginity might be a necessity in the kind of training she sought. She'd heard of such things, and not knowing what would lie ahead, she had guarded herself. She stiffened in his hold, knowing resistance was futile.

But he hesitated, whispering, "May I?"

She imagined his breath was cold on her skin. "Dorian, no. Please, no." But she did want it.

As he withdrew, she thought she saw something white and shiny concealed by the corners of his mouth. *Huge teeth?* But when his face was in moonlight again, she wasn't sure. He bowed. "Forgive my presumption."

Flustered again by the unaccustomed courtesy, she needed to escape. "I'm going to set some traps. At least we may have something to break fast on."

"Remora, I won't be joining you for breakfast." He delivered the news in the tone of a confession.

She inspected him anew. "You must have your own destination in mind. I do not hold you to any debt to me."

"I must somehow cope with the sun's rising. It's effect on me will be far more devastating than that of the water."

Cold needles of dread flashed across her skin. *Demon! Creature of the Dark.*

Her thought must have shown on her face, for he began to gather up his wet clothes. "Since it is clear that my presence distresses you, I will leave you now."

Guilt shot through her. If he was in fact a demon,

she could not let him run loose. It came to her all at once that her very presence had activated a Gate, such a portal as one only heard tales of. If he was just a man, she could not in conscience turn him out to wander and die alone. He had no food. He wore indoor shoes, and knew nothing about the countryside. Worse yet, be might not be here had she not gone into the Old Ones' place of Power.

"Please!" she called after his retreating back. "Don't go!" She ran after him.

He turned. "I will leave your blanket." His hand went to his waist.

She covered his hand with hers. "No. Wait until your clothes dry, at least." *He's just a man nearly frozen.*

He paused, a preternatural stillness overcoming him. Very quietly, as if it took great courage, he asked, "Do you mean that you may find a way to send me back?"

"Is that what you want?" A demon would want to stay.

"Yes."

"I believe you. I don't know why, but I do."

His hand slipped the cloak clasp free. "Send me back, and you may keep this."

Neave! I could buy all Mistdale for that! She searched his eyes. What demon would pay to be sent back before wreaking havoc across the land? Her hand closed over it, and he surrendered it willingly. She swallowed, throat dry. "Dorian, there is truth to be spoken."

"I know the pin's value. It's real. Keep it. It's yours."

Her hand closed over it and greed rose in her. What a

life she could have! And she had prayed for abundance and the blessing of the Old Ones' Powers. She shook her head to clear the avarice which tasted bitter on her tongue. "There is truth to be spoken," she insisted. "I may have brought you here. I'm not sure. The Gate might have opened even without me. But there is one thing every child of the Dales knows. A Gate works only one way. Nobody ever goes back."

It was so in all the tales. *But is it really true?*

"You won't even try?"

She forced the clasp back into his hand and folded his cold fingers over it. "Keep your wealth. I'll try the Gate with you once more. But you ought to learn to swim first."

He glanced at his sodden clothing. "I had forgotten. If there is a Gate, it must be at the bottom of that pool."

"No doubt. I can't believe it will function twice in one night—or even in one year. The moon has to be just right to activate the Power of the Old Ones." And she described what she had found by following the watercourse.

From the bemused expression on his face, she thought that the simplest things must be alien to him. "It must be terrible where you come from," she finished.

"It has its moments. But, no. On the whole it is beautiful." His eyes went unfocused, and he spoke in snatches as if remembering: "Snow-covered mountains, and houses with golden glowing windows...and off in the distance, the city, cupped in steep mountains...the streets outlined with chains of blue or amber lights on either side of a red stream and a white stream of pure light...the tall buildings patched with lighted windows...the blue lights of a copter pad...the winking flashes of red, yellow, and green traffic lights. There is sadness under the lights, and much tragedy, but no, it's not terrible. I suspect that here, it just may be terrible."

Colored lights. He came from a place of brightly colored light. He could not be evil. She threw her arms around him to console him. "Dorian, it's not terrible here. The world can be harsh, but it is also wonderful."

His arms went around her and she felt the soggy cloth of his garments against her back. He whispered in her ear, "If it has many as beautiful as you, it has to be wonderful. But I am afraid, Remora, that I will find no rest here."

Beautiful. As me. She squirmed free and plucked his clothes from his arm. Spreading them over the make-shift rack again, she said, "As for rest, we can build up the fire and sleep safely enough."

"It is not the practice of my kind. But I will stay and guard while you sleep. I will be gone before the dawn."

The sun. She had forgotten what he'd said of the sun. "What kind are you? You look human."

"I was. Once. But that was long ago."

"What manner of creature are you now? Of the Light—or of the Darkness?"

The ghost of a frown creased his forehead. His hesitancy to claim the Light sent a quiver of dread through her, but before he could voice his answer, a wild yammering erupted from the pass behind them.

Dorian spun to face the approaching menace, falling into a wary crouch as he swept her behind him with one long arm.

Out of the darkness loomed a churning wall of scraggly gray beasts, gaunt and long-legged four-footers. "A pack!" she gasped, knowing they had no chance against this. The runners were long-snouted, with terrible fangs.

As the leaders hesitated before the watch fire, Remora grabbed Dorian's hand, pulling him back into the rocks. "This way! The Old Ones' pool. It's our only chance!"

Tugging his hand, she ran into the defile toward the Old Ones' circle. If the fire just held the beasts long enough!

Scratched and bruised, she reached the circle and ran for the entry, knowing somehow that to gain protection she had to enter there. At the archway, she found the waning moonlight casting a shadow over the right-side pillar, and in that darkness she could still see the glowing circle.

The runes were clearer, but they were moving more slowly, sluggish now as if running out of energy.

Behind them, the baying of the pack closed in, but it was broken by occasional snarls and indignant yelps as the beasts fought among themselves. All of that faded from Remora's consciousness as she stared at the runes marching solemnly around the glowing circle. As they moved, they shifted and changed, and she fancied she could understand.

She was drawn deep into the center of the light until she saw with an inner knowledge divorced from ordinary sight. It was as if she knew this place as the builders had known it. Here was the Gate, and back there where the pack fought was the Way, a pass cut through the living rock of the mountains; the very pass she had used. But now it was crumbling and seemed a natural part of the landscape.

Off to her left had once been a small village perched atop and within the mountains. This whole region had been honeycombed with passages. Up ahead, on the other side of the Gate structure, was a cave that accessed the passages, a cave once used for food storage.

As she strained to make out what mysteries might be contained in that cave, the vision faded leaving only the knowledge that the stone circle was no longer a refuge. Its energies would not return for another century.

She came out of it with Dorian's hand clenched about her upper arm in a bruising grip. He was poised on the balls of his feet, peering back into the darkness as if he could see what approached. "Come on, Remora! Wake up!"

There was movement in the shadows behind them, and flashes of gleaming white teeth, glowing eyes. "This way!" she whispered, and yanked him along into the circle.

They skirted the pond which was cold and dark now. Behind them, the beasts gathered at the gateway, milling about in confusion, yammering as if gathering courage for a final assault. *The power will only last a few more moments.*

"Run!" she urged Dorian.

They skinned through a narrow slit between two uprights, and clamored up the other side of the cup that held the circle. Skidding, smothering yelps at twisted ankles and scraped shins, they climbed.

"Here!" she gasped. "It has to be here!"

"What has to be here?" asked Dorian, surveying the tumbled mess of boulders before them. Small twisted bushes, and stunted trees dotted the crumbled cliff. Outlined blackly against the moonlight, they seemed menacing.

With a shiver of foreboding, Remora scrambled frantically up the cliff, searching. "A cave mouth. It'll be safe. The runners won't go very deep into a cave."

"How do you know?"

I hope! "The circle told me."

He only nodded. Then he climbed straight up the side of a large boulder, topped it, and stood peering into the inky blackness above. His head swept right and left, like a hunting serpent.

She watched, overcome with the matter-of-fact way he had accepted her explanation. No one had ever done that before. She didn't pause in her search, scanning the jumbled shadows for a dark opening. She knew just what it had to look like, and that, she concluded later, was why she missed it.

"There! A cave!" His whisper was harsh with suppressed excitement. A moment later, she never knew how, he appeared beside her without a sound.

"Come on, I'll help you."

Now, he chose a slanted path, cutting back and forth to find solid footing as if he could see perfectly. He gripped her arm above the elbow, and her fingers closed on his wrist. His strength was phenomenal. She felt as if he levitated her up the difficult rises. And he wasn't even panting when they reached a small, wedge-shaped hole between two boulders.

It wasn't anything like the spacious entry she had seen. But then neither was the broken cliff like what she had seen.

They wriggled through the hole and found the space opened out around them. Only then did she think that they should have brought some dry wood to build a fire in the cave mouth to discourage the runners until dawn drove them away. Failing so much, they could still have used a brand or two from the fire to make a torch. *Stupid!*

"Well, there's no choice. We'll have to go that way."

"I can't see a thing."

"But you can smell, can't you?"

There was a repellent odor lingering on the air. "Something probably denned here. Let's hope it's not home."

He took a cautious step forward, holding onto her fingers to pull her along into the dark. Their feet crunched something foul as they stepped. "Bats!" he spat.

"What?"

"I don't know what you call them, but they're harmless. That's not what I smell." His face flashed whitely as he glanced back toward the dim glow of the entry. "I don't want to go down there."

"There should be a long tunnel that opens out into a large chamber, and another tunnel on the other side that leads out to the open air beyond."

He took another cautious step forward. "The circle told you?" His tone was not the slightest bit mocking.

"The Old Ones, who built the circle...I know what it was like when it was built and used. They stored food in this cave."

"How long ago was that?"

"Uncounted centuries."

"Then that can't be the smell."

As they ventured forward, picking their way carefully over the dung, she felt the shudder of revulsion rippling through him. Her own gorge was rising, and she gagged.

"Maybe we won't have to go very much farther. The stench has to repel the creatures chasing us."

"Maybe." If not, it'd be better to face the relatively clean death the beasts would give than to go on into that!

Still, she was not ready to give up her life or her chance to find Arvon. *Evil can be vanquished. I hope.*

Her ears told her they were in a narrow tunnel now. Progress became a nightmare of endurance. She clenched her jaw, her breath hissing between her teeth, feet leaden.

She forced her mind to narrow down to the image of

the way out that had to lie ahead of them. It had to be there still. *Just keep going*, she told herself, *and we'll get there somehow. I'm not going to let this stop me.*

She had nearly lost touch with everything else but that one determined thought when they rounded a curve, and suddenly found themselves in a wide chamber. But now it was filled with a sickening bluish glow, and the odor became a vile miasma that gagged Remora. She couldn't breathe.

She'd barely glimpsed the walls of the cave, festooned with shapeless lumps of something foul, when Dorian turned and pushed her back. "God! Let's get out of here. We can't get through that!"

Retreating into the dark, she clung to him for a moment, digging in her heels to stop the huge man in his tracks. His arms came around her in a protective gesture, and something in her responded sharply. But this was not the time for that. She pushed away. "Listen. We can't go back. The way out has got to be ahead."

"Better the wolves than that. Something ghastly has grown out of whatever the Old Ones left here. Besides, that was so long ago that the other tunnel may have been crushed by now. Something has changed this place. I mean, you don't ordinarily store food where the walls drip water!"

She thought about it. The mountain had shifted. He was right. "We can't go back," she repeated. "It's not long until dawn. Maybe if we wait here?"

He cast a glance toward the softly glowing turn in the

passage. "I can't. Whatever happened here, Remora, it was an evil thing. I cannot, I will not abide here."

That spoke to something so deep in her she found herself retreating before him despite her resolve. And in that defeat she also found a leap of triumph in her breast, a relief of a tension she'd forgotten was there. He's not of the Dark! If he was, he'd have found that place like home.

At a wider spot in the tunnel, he squeezed by her, his blanket-clad body against hers, and she felt him trembling. Something here repelled him even more strongly than it did her. When he took the lead again, he drew her along with such speed that she was hard put to keep from stumbling.

The way back seemed longer than the way in. Eventually, though they heard the disconsolate baying of the pack, echoes multiplying their numbers.

At last, he paused. Putting both huge hands on her shoulders, he brought his face close to hers so she could feel his cool breath on her face. "You wait here. If they smell you, they'll attack. There's a chance, maybe it's an outside chance, but worth a try, that I can send them away even before dawn. I'm willing to risk it, but you've got to give me time. Wait until I call you."

His instruction was delivered in that calm, commanding tone she had obeyed all of her life. She whispered, "Very well," and stopped herself before adding lord. "Dorian. Be careful. You don't know how vicious they can be."

"On my world, there are creatures much like these

called wolves. When they're hungry, very little will stop them."

"Oh, these runners are hungry. They're always hungry. And they love human flesh."

"Good. Then I may have an advantage."

And then he was gone into the darkness.

She waited. Her ears brought her nothing except the snuffling and arguing of the pack. Once he was beyond arm's reach, she heard not a whisper of movement from Dorian.

She waited an eternity, and there was nothing. Her mind showed her Dorian lying unconscious, fallen in the dark. Then she saw the runners, catching his scent, and attacking his helpless form, not even baying their triumph as the man was unconscious and hardly more than carrion. The constant murmuring of the pack she heard could be them feeding. Vision or imagination? She'd never seen anything from current time before, but then most people who saw did see in the present, too. She had to go check.

It took less courage to creep toward the pack than it had to stumble into that horrible odor. Bracing one hand on the wall, she shuffled and groped toward the entry.

The last rays of the setting moon combined with the first hint of false dawn made the entry seem bright before Remora's eyes. As she neared the end of the tunnel, where it opened into the wider chamber inside the entry, she made out Dorian's form, prone at the mouth of the tunnel, just as she'd seen. His head was toward the entry, his feet to her, and his face was buried in his elbow.

Beyond his head, not three body-lengths away, gray shapes paced and wheeled, grumbling though not feasting on Dorian. But he'd said the sun's rays were deadly to his kind. With his ability to see in the dark, she didn't doubt that sun would hurt his eyes.

As she crept up to Dorian's feet, the pack became more agitated. Milling faster, they edged toward him, threatening growls rumbling as teeth bared. She saw his chest rise. *He's not dead!* A runner snapped at her, snarling.

Flinching, she realized she was about to cause the very vision she had feared. And when they finished with Dorian, they'd turn on her. Before she could do anything, Dorian gathered himself and rose soundlessly to his full height. His white face was frozen in a forbidding mask as he snarled out of the side of his mouth, "Idiot! I told you to wait! They're not wolves, but I almost had them!"

As he said this, the leader of the pack leaped into the air, hurtling at her. Rooted to the spot, she braced herself to die but her hands came up to ward those awful teeth away from her throat. Suddenly she was staring into Dorian's partially blanketed back.

She felt rather than saw the animal's impact on Dorian, and heard something issue from Dorian's throat that wasn't at all human. And then he was pushing forward into the pack.

Dorian heaved the pack leader among his fellows

and snarled at them in a command that could not be disobeyed.

Dorian continued to advance, animals whirling about his knees, venturing to snap at his heels and the edges of his cloak. He grabbed the leader by the scruff of the neck and threw him toward the entry, snarling commands.

One of the runners dared snap at Dorian's hand, gouging the flesh beneath the thumb. Instead of withdrawing the injured member, Dorian made a fist and punched the offending animal in the nose. It whimpered and retreated.

At that, the leader slunk toward the entry, and the pack followed, bellies to the ground, tails between their legs. Slowly, as the sun rose outside, the animals lowered their front paws over the lip of the cave mouth, found purchase, and, one by one, crawled out into the daylight they hated.

Dorian, still trembling, lips compressed, blocked their access to Remora, driving them out into the light.

And the sun rose. Relentlessly the light increased.

But Dorian refused to give ground. Occasionally he had to lash at one of the reluctant runners. By the time the last had crawled out onto the tumbled mountainside, the sun, had obliterated the stars, and diffuse light reached almost to Dorian's feet. Dorian edged back, squinting at the glowing triangle of the entry.

"Let me look out. The light must hurt your eyes."

He let her edge by and crawl to the lip of the cave. The last of the runners picked their way carefully down the broken cliff face. They had the skill and grace of the mountain-born, and she found herself hoping she'd not have to face anything like them out on the Waste.

When the last stragglers were down, they ran in circles baying their defiance, and then they took off into the dawn.

"It's all right," she called back. "They're gone."

When there was no answer, she turned to find him still as a statue in the same spot where she'd left him. Her shadow stretched out behind her, but sunlight had crept onto his legs. His face and hands seemed to glow in the light.

He was staring at his hands. The spot where he'd been bitten was unmarred. Not even a drop of blood remained. He knelt, moving slowly like a person in shock, not quite sure if his body was still real. He thrust his hands into a puddle of light as if he expected they'd dissipate in smoke. Nothing happened.

A puzzled frown creased his brow, and he opened the other hand in the light, palm up. His cupped hands caught the light as if it were water. Worried, Remora wriggled back into the cave and stood. "Come on, Dorian, we have to find you a place to spend the day."

He didn't move, and she went to lift him up and urge him back into the darkness. If this was what a little light did to him, she didn't want to see what would happen in full sun. "Come on, I'll help you."

He came to his feet, staring at his hands. Then his eyes rose to her face. "Remora! The sun..."

"You told me. It's not good for you. It's all right. I

know you're of the Light now."

He took her by the shoulders. "It doesn't hurt! Didn't you see! It doesn't hurt. The sun here must be different!"

She frowned. "The sun is the sun."

He padded over to the entry and knelt, worming up to the lip as she had done. His bulk filled the little triangle, cutting off the light, but his voice came back to her with a joyous shout. "It doesn't hurt! It doesn't burn!"

Then his feet disappeared over the lip, as he went out headfirst as the animals had done.

Thinking he'd fallen, she scrambled to the lip to peer out again, and found him clinging to the boulders outside the cave. He had reversed handily and his head was now level with hers. "Remora, come! Let's dance in the sunlight! I'm going to love your world!"

If it gave him the freedom of the day, she could understand that. "All right, give me some room."

But he didn't move. His eyes had gone to her scratched and bleeding hands, ravaged by the night's heedless flight. His tongue danced over his lips, which seemed parched and cracked. He whispered, "One thing, though, hasn't changed."

Quivering, his lips clamped shut and his mouth narrowed into a thin line. His eyes moved up to meet hers, and she felt his hunger lance through her like a hot knife.

Behind that peculiar sensation came a call that stirred her to untold depths. Her lips parted and she could hardly breathe with the need that seized her. She knew only that she had to come into his arms or life would be intolerable forevermore. She started to move, to answer that call.

Suddenly, as fast as it had come, it was gone.

"No. I won't."

In moves so fast they blurred, he went straight down the cliff, heedless of the broken terrain. She knew she could never catch him, but she backed back into the cave as fast as she could, reversed, and dangled her feet over the lip of the entry until she found purchase. By the time she reached the bottom, he was out of sight. There was no sign of his passage, and in desperation, she raised her voice and called out, "Dorian! Dorian! Don't go!"

She listened to her words echo and wondered why she didn't want to be free of him. Still, he'd saved her life, and now she realized it had been done at no small risk to his own. He hadn't known he could bully the runners into leaving, and he'd known dawn was close. He'd thought the sun would kill him, and even so, he'd defied that death to chase the pack from her. "Dorian! Don't go! Please! Dorian!"

She made her way back to the circle, and found him sitting beside the pond bathing his hands. He glanced up, and she saw he had water cupped in his hands. The look of desperation on his face frightened her, but she was too far away to do or say anything when he abruptly thrust his face into his hands and drank, as if taking poison.

His throat convulsed with forced swallowing, and again his pale oval face raised to hers. She stood rooted to the spot until he caved in, and curled up clutching his stomach.

He started to vomit, and she ran toward him. Her foot turned on a rock and she stumbled sideways. After that, she went carefully, and by the time she reached him, he was bent over, sobbing quietly. The mess on the turf before him reeked in a way she'd never known vomit to. "You're ill. Dorian, trust me. I'll take care of you."

He shook his head.

"Look, you've had a nasty shock just getting here, a bad chill, and then the runners. Come back to camp and I'll make you some broth."

He shook his head again, and gathered himself up.

She tried to help him to his feet, talking as one would to someone delirious with fever, but he cut her off. He grabbed her hands and pulled them up between them, as if to show them to her.

As a confession wrenched from one in the throes of great remorse, words came from him, one at a time. "Remora, it isn't broth I crave. It's blood. Your blood. My kind live on the blood of humans."

He flung her hands down, turned, and strode off.

She stood in shock, adding up all the clues that had lain before her through the night. Blood. She shuddered. How could any creature of the Light live on blood?

And yet.

He had wanted her blood. He had wanted it from the moment they'd met. He had been hungry when he came through the Gate. And he had never, ever, made one move to take what he hungered for. She remembered the look on his face when he'd swallowed the water. He'd hoped that, too, was over.

"Dorian!" She ran after him. "Dorian, stop." She caught him at the edge of the cup that held the circle. Pulling him to a halt, she made him turn to face her. "I owe you my life. Is it my life that you want?"

"No! No, I will never harm you. I gave that pledge when you saved me from the water. I have saved your life, and we're even, no? You go your way, and I'll go mine."

"See me safely across the Waste," she challenged, "as you said would be proper, and you can have some of my blood."

Stunned, he just stared at her.

"The sun won't harm you. You can travel the Waste to Arvon. There are still Old Ones there. Maybe they can find a way to help you learn to eat normal food again."

"Old Ones? Alive?"

"Maybe. I've heard people say they know people who've seen them. They're supposed to live very long lives, centuries even. I'm going there to learn from them."

"Centuries?" He repeated avidly.

"Dorian, come with me."

"Across the Waste?" His face turned in that direction.

"Why not? Where else in this world have you got to go."

"Well..."

It all seemed so clear to her. They had to go together. She glanced back at the circle, knowing that the Great Powers ruled there. What they brought into a life couldn't easily be refused. All at once, she raised her bleeding hands to his mouth, commanding, "Drink!"

His resistance cracked. His tongue came out to lick her wounds, and she trembled at the gentleness she sensed through that touch. His hands rose to hers, and his eyes came to focus on her own. Warm thrills coursed through her nerves, promises too sweet to ever be fulfilled. But this time, there was no raw compulsion behind it.

Sometime later, he lowered her hands, put one arm around her shoulders, and urged her back toward camp. "Not like this. Come, and I'll show you how it's done. You won't be disappointed, Remora. I promise."

Afterword for "Through the Moon Gate"

I chose to tell of the first vampire to be swept into the Witch World because at the time Andre asked for the contribution, I was ruminating over a vampire novel. I was reading and studying about the phenomenon, much taken with Yarbro's St. Germaine and other "good" vampires in the current literature.

I had selected for my novels *Those of My Blood* and *Dreamspy*, a particular theory of vampirism which allowed for a war between the good and bad vampires on Earth all without magic involved, but that by no means exhausted my ideas.

When Andre finally confirmed her interest in the basic idea providing that the individual I chose to bring to her Witch World universe were of the "good" persuasion, I gleefully created a magical vampire and wrote "Through the Moon Gate."

I had a rousing good time figuring how the laws of the Witch World reality might affect the "curse" of my vampire. I think he's going to like living (sic) in this new reality, and I now expect he'll survive the Warding to return to Earth where strange loves await him.

All my "good" vampires tend to fall passionately in love with only one human at a time, and of course always at the most inconvenient time possible.

FALSE PROPHECY

"False Prophecy" is a prequel to the novel *Those of My Blood* by Jacqueline Lichtenberg. Here the vampires are not supernatural, though an ordinary human might not notice that. http://www.simegen.com/jl/ for info.

Oh, I hope I'm doing the right thing!
Bringing her Mazda to a stop at the red light, Gavriella Dean peered up at the rusty highway signs overhead barely lit by the street lamps. Route 59 East, ahead. Route 9W South, to the right.

Yes, this had to be the corner. With New York's crazy right turn laws, she couldn't figure out if she could turn against the red light or not, so she sat there visualizing the Hanged Man Tarot card, suppressing a touch of hysteria. She'd never read Tarot in public before, and to start at a Halloween costume party seemed, well, risky.

Thy Will be done, she prayed, placing her destiny in the hands of God, and made the turn. Maybe she wouldn't find the house. Then she could just go home.

9W climbed and narrowed to a crumbling, two way track lined with tumble-down businesses. Then she passed the sign that said, THE NYACKS' HISTORICAL PRESERVATION AREA, and suddenly there were gorgeous Victorian homes on either side of the road, with carefully painted gingerbread, turrets, and roofed carriage porches on the sides.

Ordinarily, she supposed, this area would be beautiful, especially when lit by the perfect full moon now climbing the sky. But many of the houses were decorated for Halloween, some whimsically, some sinisterly. The animated holos of ghosts, witches, and vampires got to her, but she resisted closing her eyes as she passed them. She had been warned.

She counted streets and landmarks according to her directions. Before she knew it, the land to her left dropped away and the road became a narrow ledge cut into the hillside, treetops and roof turrets poking up next to her car. Over them, she could see the Hudson River, and beyond, the dense lights of the city.

Dirt driveways snaked up the steep hillside on her right, and twisted down to the houses buried under the trees on her left. Racks of mail boxes were stationed at intervals. Some were decorated with jack-o-lanterns or ghosts. She almost missed the one she was hunting for right under a holo of a red-eyed vampire bat. But, just beyond it a line of cars was parked against the cliff, left tires barely clear of the white line that edged the roadway. She tucked her Mazda in behind a Lincoln and doused the lights.

Shouldering her bag, she dragged the lace shawl of her makeshift witch's costume around her and walked back to the stairs up to the house. The narrow stair was cut into the solid rock. Modern lights lit the treads and banister, but the stairs looked more than a century old.

She put her head down and climbed, praying *If You're sure this is what You want, okay.* She was visualizing The Hermit card, staff and lantern lighting her climb to Wisdom, when feet scuffed to a stop beyond her nose.

A man gasped, "Oh! Sorry!" and backed up the narrow stair.

Simultaneously, she backed down, barely stifling a yelp, and had to grab the banister. The stair treads were an odd and irregular height and worn unevenly. Suddenly, she was falling backwards.

Hands closed over her arms and she was lifted back up the steps and set down on a landing edged with shrubbery on both sides. She'd never been lifted like that before; all hundred seventy-seven pounds of her five-foot-two body just moved. It made her feel like a ballerina, beautiful and graceful, until she heard the man grunt with the effort as if he'd strained himself.

Heart pounding, she looked up at her benefactor, a slender young man in a Dracula costume with a rental tag showing at the collar. In one electric glance, she took in the blood red satin lined cape, archaic tuxedo and pale white makeup on hands and face that was so well done, it didn't look like makeup at all. The moon glancing off his eyes had struck ruby highlights somehow. It absolutely made the outfit. "Red contacts, right?" she gasped.

He laughed. It was a wonderfully rich sound. "Right. I'm sorry I startled you. My name is Titus Shiddehara."

"Gabby. Short for Gavriella. Gavriella Dean." Her voice was choked and husky, and she thought she might faint.

"Here," said Titus drawing her through the bushes, "come over here and catch your breath. It's still along climb up to the house and witches shouldn't arrive out of breath."

Against her better judgment, her feet followed him into the bushes which were so thick with vines that the wall of growth closed up behind her.

But then they were on a moonlit lawn under a gnarled oak that had to be a century old. Behind them, the windows of the house spilled out light, music and shrieks that turned to laughter. Behind the house, the hillside rose steeply, covered with trees and vines. The only exposed spot was a huge rock that stuck out of the hill, forming a kind of overlook. She could just discern the hint of a foot path that disappeared into the under-growth, probably leading to the rock.

She couldn't imagine why anyone would go up there. There was no retaining wall around the edge of the rock.

She surveyed the river and the city beyond. The velvet dark was sprinkled with jewels and presided over by the moon which made golden paths on the river. Like a Tarot card.

Titus said with restrained disapproval, "I have to warn you the entire climb from here up to the house is trapped with fun house tricks, some pretty realistic ones, too. Brace yourself, and don't get startled like that again."

She stepped away to get a better look at him. "You were leaving?" She'd arrived a quarter hour early.

"I didn't care for the atmosphere. The whole house is filled with things that pop out of closets or swoop down from the shadows of the high ceilings. And there are a few people doing drugs already." He flashed her a smile. "I don't suppose I could offer to take you to a movie, or something?"

He hadn't laid a finger on her since he'd dragged her into the bushes. "I'm tempted. Doesn't sound like my kind of party, either. But I gave my word. I'm supposed to be reading Tarot to entertain the guests." Tarot wouldn't work if they were into drugs already, so she was really tempted to leave.

"Do you read at a lot of parties?"

"No. I'm just doing this as a favor to my boss. I've been reading for other people for about a year, but not at parties." She pulled the lace shawl up, wishing she'd come in a business suit instead of letting her sister talk her into the costume. At least she'd have been warmer.

"Gabby, they've already got a lot of readers. I don't think they'd miss you."

"Maybe I can get away early. But I really have to do a couple of hours at least. I did promise."

There was a squirming discomfort in her stomach, a warning she was about to do something she'd regret. She never picked up strange guys. That was how women became police statistics.

But when she'd consulted the cards over coming to this party, the theme that ran through every layout was Hanged Man, Hermit, and Lovers; putting trust in the Higher Powers, following the path to Maturity, and facing temptations or finding real inner harmony through relationships.

But there'd also been a number of Fives tangled through the whole issue, along with the Nine and Ten of Swords. Whatever was due to happen would hurt a lot. But she'd learned long since that challenges like that led to worthwhile triumphs.

"Well," allowed Titus, "in that case, I'll wait." He guided her back onto the stairs, warning her of hidden obstacles he'd tripped over when he'd discovered the secluded spot. They went up the long, long stair together, Titus alerting her at each trap. She didn't tell him how much she appreciated his help, and then immediately regretted it when he delivered her to the door and vanished into the crowd.

Oddly enough, despite the cobwebs and skeletons décor, Gabby's queasy discomfort vanished also. *That man's the temptation I'm here to resist.* She could already tell that resisting wasn't going to be easy.

The host, the man who had financed her boss's venture into newspaper publishing, was standing in the entry foyer beside a real, satin lined, teak coffin wearing a fabulous Dracula costume, complete with appropriate dentition. But she'd never seen a Dracula with gray hair, spectacles, and an ample waistline before. *Well, why not?*

As she introduced herself, Gabby realized that Titus had lacked the fangs, but their host had omitted the contacts.

She'd been told there was to be a Dracula contest later. There were already ten or fifteen Draculas in the living room behind the man she was facing.

"Ms. Dean?"

"Uh, yes sir?" The unmistakable odor of pot wafted through the spray-can-cobwebs. *Well, if it's just pot...*

"Please follow Mr. Simon. He'll show you to the room we've prepared for you." He intoned the words with silken menace, and laughed diabolically, then turned to the couple entering behind Gabby, Dracula-and-night-gowned-victim.

He was really enjoying the act, she realized, as she followed the man in the caterer's outfit. As she saw others wearing identical black jumpsuits with red cummerbunds carrying white towels over their left arms, passing large trays among the guests, she realized he was a real waiter, not a costumed guest. *I'm way out of my class here!*

Installed in what had been a small bedroom, decorated now as a gypsy tent complete with little round table and crystal ball, she ordered a virgin Mary, then cleared the crystal ball off the table. It was a real one, probably costing more than she made in a week as a features editor. She put it on the floor in the corner and tucked it behind a fold of the cloth which draped the walls. She discovered a small attic window and grunted it open a crack. The cramped room was already stuffy.

Then she saw the antique china bowl on a side table by the door. A huge sign over it, shaped like a hand raised in benediction, read, CROSS MY PALM WITH SILVER AND I'LL REVEAL YOUR FUTURE.

Oh-my-God!

She yanked the sign off the table so hard the whole table collapsed. She grabbed the bowl just in time, and discovered the table was just a folding cardboard parson's table draped with a round cloth. She set it up again and put the bowl back upside down.

A gypsy woman swirled into the room, beads rattling. Immediately, her hands went out to right the bowl. "Cheesy little tables. You'd think a place like this could afford better props! What happened to your sign?"

"Excuse me?" Gabby had no idea who the woman could be.

"I work next door here. Cynthia. Where's your sign? They did give you one?"

"Uh, look, I don't do this for money. Ever."

Cynthia's whole demeanor changed. Gabby retreated a bit, sensing she'd offended the woman. Then Cynthia put one arm around her shoulders and said confidentially, "Look, if you take that attitude, you'll undercut the trade. It makes us all look bad, especially if you're any good. Are you?"

"Well, my clients keep coming back...."

"So. You are good. Well. You know, it's all right to take money for a Reading if it's the only way you can support yourself, which is the way it is for most of us here. And these kind of people, well. They're not going to listen to free advice. If they have to pay for it, what you tell them will make an impression. You do tell the truth, don't you?"

"Yes," she answered uncertainly.

"You wouldn't want it ignored just because you sold it cheap?"

"No."

"So. There. You see? That's settled. Where did you say that sign was?"

"I'll, uh, I'll take care of what needs to be done."

Summoning all the courage she'd ever owned, Gabby ushered the woman out the door. People were milling around in the hall, comparing the readings they'd been given.

Cynthia disappeared into the throng, and Gabby snatched the little table and folded it up, hiding the bowl underneath the heap of material, hoping it would blend into the décor. Then she asked a blessing and protection for her working space.

She wouldn't take money. She had a job, though she might not have tomorrow morning if she just picked up and left the party now. She was behind in her car payments and had no idea how she'd scrape together next month's rent, but her teachers had warned her repeatedly of the dangers of going commercial.

A voice asked, "Are you reading?"

It was a woman with too much makeup and too little dress covering her hips. But other than that, she looked normal. "Yes," said Gabby, "I was about to start."

The woman held her drink away and turned to display the red sequined outfit. "Like it? I'm the Virgin Victim of Dracula. His cape is lined with the same red sequins."

"Oh. Very impressive." She wondered how many "virgin victims" the Draculas had brought. Gabby settled at the round table and spread out her silk reading cloth, then began shuffling her cards. "Have you ever had a Tarot reading before?" There was no alcohol on the woman's breath. At least there was a chance this one reading would work.

So the evening began. Before and after each reading, Gabby had to explain that there was no charge, that if the reading proved of value, then the recipient could make a donation to their own favorite charity, but even that wasn't necessary. She got very tired of that speech.

Three clients and an hour later, she had to ask for a NO SMOKING sign. After that, she fell into the natural trance in which she did her best reading, and words started to flow as the gestalt pattern of each card layout became perfectly clear.

Words flowed from her, describing by analogy and anecdote, explaining by parables she originated on the spot, elaborating and embroidering on each card's inner meaning for those who would listen. And a moment after she picked up the cards to reshuffle, she had forgotten what she'd said.

The clients made little impression on her. They were patterns in the cards, classic problems in living life, layers and crosscurrents of power struggles in domestic affairs, knotty choices of vocation or job, serious quests for spiritual enlightenment.

At one point she realized she needed to use two different decks, so she moved onto the floor where she could sit in lotus and spread out the work. taking the most portentous card from the first layout as significator for a second reading, she used the deck she had drawn and colored herself for the second reading. Comparing the two readings, she could penetrate the mists of the client's subconscious, and finally understand where the anguish was coming from.

"No, that's not what you want," Gabby said. "That's what others want of you. What is it you, yourself, need?"

The client, a young, skinny woman dressed as a Dracula, broke into sobs. "You're right! My God, you're right!"

Gabby looked up and realized she had a huge audience peering down at them. "Somebody get a box of tissues." Then she put her arm around the client and talked her back to composure. It took six tissues. She'd hit a nerve.

The onlookers had been friends of the client, most of them privy to the actual problem. Gabby, herself, didn't know and didn't want to know the personal details. "It's all right to kibitz, and it's even good to watch if you've never seen this done before. All I can do is describe the general pattern of the seeker's current life-crisis. I can't reveal anything really private. I can't foretell the future. I can only describe the decisions already made, where they might lead, and the options still open. I can't even tell what's the best solution. I can only describe the problem in terms of the value system inherent in the Tarot."

"Can I go next?" asked someone.

"Certainly." It was a young man in a Harlequin suit who folded his long legs tailor fashion and sat next to her.

After that, she lost track. The crowd around her never thinned, and though many broke into astonished sobs during the readings, there was never a lack of volunteers. As usual with a group, the readings began to fall into a pattern echoing her own most recent pattern, of Hanged Man/Hermit/Lovers laced with varying combinations of 5's and the themes of the 9 and 10 of Swords.

As the crowd around her had heard her repeat the instructions to the seeker many times, she eventually left them out.

It was close to midnight, and she had just organized the people waiting into a line, promising to get to them in order when one of the waiters brought her another Virgin Mary and announced, "Ms. Dean, it's time for your break." He raised his voice. "She's entitled to half an hour now."

Suddenly, there was a space around her, and contrite murmurings of how tired she must be. Very quickly, the room emptied. Actually, she felt no strain. She was, however, stiff from sitting so long, and she discovered she'd been sitting in the cold draft from the window. It felt good to get up and move. And then she saw the table by the door.

The bowl was back in place, and it was half full of currency, tens, twenties, and even a few crisp hundreds. It looked like more than a month's salary.

What am I going to do?

Not even wanting to touch it, she pushed out into the crowded hall where people were milling about or waiting in line at the other doors. Some of the Draculas now wore prize ribbons pinned to their lapels.

She found the lavatory when someone came out. She went in, glad that her makeup, wallet and necessaries were in a leather pouch tied to her waste, part of the medieval flavor of the witch's costume. Refreshed, she emerged to find their host was working up and down the hall, making sure everyone was happy. He seemed to be enjoying himself immensely.

She plastered herself against the wall to let him pass, but he spotted her. "Ah, Ms. Dean, you've become quite a hit!" He reached into his breast pocket and produced an elegantly printed envelope which he presented to her. "Your fee. Only a token compared to what you've been collecting."

Pushing the envelope away, she shook her head. He drew her hand up and curled it around the envelope. It was a thick package. "I'm so grateful to Tom for getting you to come. You're worth more than any of the others. I won't forget the favor." With a raised eyebrow and a nod, he was gone into the crowd.

Clutching the envelope, stunned, she felt large, strong hands came onto her shoulders, kneading the tension she hadn't realized was there. She stifled a yelp, and spun to find Titus behind her. "Oh! You shouldn't do that!"

"I think you need it. You've been working harder than anyone, and with far better results. Ready to leave yet?"

"Oh, I can't." *This man is the temptation I have to resist.* But there had never been all that many personable men interested in her.

"Listen, Gabby," he said leaning over to speak softly into her ear as he worked on her back, "some people here are dealing. This is a Wall Street crowd, very high class, very elegant, but still, the place could be raided. I don't want to get caught in anything like that and neither do you."

"Dealing," she repeated, stricken. She turned and noted inanely that the rental tag was gone from his collar.

She wanted to grab her Tarot bag and go. It was plausible that someone here would be dealing. She'd done many readings indicative of substance and power abuse. Still, she hadn't seen it with her own eyes, and this man was the temptation she had to resist. He'd certainly found her most sensitive button, too.

He was just the sort of man no sane woman would get involved with; so sexy she could hardly stand it, so insightful he found her buttons before they'd even had a single date, and so manipulative he'd push those buttons shamelessly. What sort of marriage could that lead to? Besides, she didn't want to get married. She was a career woman on the way up. Wasn't she?

"Titus," she said, knowing she should keep it formal but unable to remember his last name, "I can't. I promised at least ten more people."

"You should make them come to your office."

"What?"

"Good psychologists don't give away free samples."

"Oh, no. You've got it all wrong." She explained she was only a features editor for an Advertiser distributed free to home owners in Bergen County, just across in New Jersey.

He eyed the knot of people beginning to collect outside her door and the fervent, animated discussions developing among them. "I'd say you're in the wrong line of work."

"Titus, people always behave this way about the Tarot because the results run so completely counter to everything we think we know about reality. The Tarot works. Come on, try it, you'll see."

This time she took his hand and tugged him through a barrier, not shrubbery but people. It parted before them and closed behind them. As she entered the room, she tossed the envelope into the bowl, noticing that there was as much in there now as there had been when she'd left the room. She realized she'd vaguely hoped somebody would steal it.

The floor had been cleaned up, and her things were set up on the table again. She shrugged. She had, out of habit, put all her cards away and wrapped them, so there was no harm done. Titus went with her as far as the client's seat, but as she moved around the table, he balked.

"No, no. This is ridiculous."

"Suspend your disbelief," she suggested.

"I'm an astrophysicist here for a convention. This just doesn't fit my concept of reality. Not at all."

Maybe that's what's so strange about his aura. She realized the queasy feeling was back again. Perhaps it meant he was a heavily repressed psychic, or a deeply disturbed person. There was no denying the rich sexual attraction she felt, but it would be a bad mistake to get involved, especially knowing how incompatible they were. Besides, if he was not from around here, she'd never see him again after tonight. She was glad she'd declined to go out with him.

Then she looked up at him, and he was looking down at her as if she were beautiful. She had to say something or she'd seem to be staring. "Why aren't you wearing a prize ribbon? You're certainly the best Dracula I've seen."

She was immediately embarrassed at what her mouth had said of its own accord, but he responded levelly, "I didn't expect to stay for the contest, but I'm glad I did."

"Oh, why?" She was enjoying just being near him and despite the cluster of people politely hanging back by the door, she wanted to prolong the experience.

"I hadn't realized so many more Draculas would turn up."

It wasn't the flirtatious response she'd expected. "Are you a connoiseur of Draculas?"

"No, I was just looking for someone. He hasn't come, and the atmosphere is even worse now. Are you sure you wouldn't like to go somewhere for coffee? There's a Denny's up on Rt. 59."

She was ready to go simply because he hadn't invited her to a bar or a dance hall. Temptation. "Titus, I hate to point this out, but I'm part of that distasteful atmosphere. I don't think you'd really care for the company of someone who interprets the world in terms of occult principles."

"No, no!" Leaning closer, he said confidentially, "The atmosphere I referred to was the alcohol and drugs, and the people who need that to have fun or make fortunes trading on others' weaknesses. It is dangerous to stay here."

"Then I guess you'd better go. I did promise the others in line."

He withdrew. She was overwhelmed with a sudden regret and had to grit her teeth not to call out to him. He paused and turned back to her, frowned, then said, "I'll just watch you work for a while. Okay?"

He wants to protect me! It wasn't the way most men reacted to her, and it felt oddly thrilling to be so valued. But then she took another look at him as he turned to inspect the crowd. Sideways, he looked like Frank Sinatra in the oldest movies, so thin a strong wind would blow him over. Mafia Muscle wouldn't even notice him. But even that cynical observation couldn't erase the thrill warming her inside.

Then a black woman in a diaphanous ghost costume complete with clanking chains came forward. Gabby remembered the costume and began shuffling.

The work picked up as it had left off, and she forgot all about Titus. Occasionally, though, as one client left and another sat down, there would be a break in the wall of bodies through which she glimpsed someone putting money in her bowl. She began to wonder if she could take it all home. Maybe, if it was still there at the end of the evening it would mean she was properly entitled to it. After all, she'd never done so many readings in a row, nor worked so hard at them, nor had she ever been so fiendishly accurate.

She began to enjoy the working a new way. A peculiar gratification swept through her each time she spread out the cards and drew forth a precise statement of the problem. At some point, the queasiness denoting Titus's presence vanished but she hardly noticed. She'd hit a breakthrough in her skills. For the first time in her life, she felt she was worth any amount of money, praise or respect offered her. And she saw that as she became more accurate, her clients left more money in the bowl. She could see a mound of green paper heaping above the rim.

Aware of the spellbound awe of her audience, she began to strive to increase the effect. Occasionally, now, she began to miss. One client simply could not make sense of what she said, and with another, she found the cards would not synthesize into a meaning.

But even when she had to give up, disappointing a client, others came forward eagerly.

They were on the third box of tissues, and the crowd had thinned, the dull roar of noise from down stairs having abated significantly, when five burly Draculas stalked into the room. Three of them spread out as one approached the empty client's chair. Unobtrusively, people drifted out of the room, but Gabby hardly noticed when the last of them left her alone with the four men.

Through the open window she heard doors clattering and cars starting up, people laughing and calling to each other.

The man before her reached in to his breast pocket, fumbling with the ribbon and pendant of a replica of a Royal Order, and brought out six one-thousand dollar bills. He placed three of the bills on the table before her. "It seems you can actually do this witch stuff. So tell me what's going to happen at 4 a.m. today, and the other three bills are yours, too." He fingered the bills he still held.

I could be completely out of debt. I could afford to go back to school. But she said, "The Tarot can't predict the future."

He leaned closer, looming over her. "Now you and I both know that's not true. You've already done it accurately for several people tonight." He exuded the same kind of quiet menace that her boss and other powerful men did. It didn't mean he was the one who was dealing. It could be about some insider trading on the Tokyo exchange.

She swallowed hard, her mouth dry. *Suppose I can't do it? Or suppose I get it all wrong?*

He moved the deck of cards in front of her. "Do it."

Hands shaking, she shuffled the cards and set them down for him to cut, muttering the instructions with her mouth while her mind was frantically invoking Protection. The familiar routine steadied her hands and the shroud of the reading trance settled over her. She snapped each card face up on the table in a Celtic Cross. The pattern coalesced as crisp and clear as any she'd seen that night.

Devil crossed by the Tower, with the Moon beneath and the Page of Swords behind.

He's dealing drugs and there's a spy in his organization who's set him up.

Violence, shocking revelations. It was just supposition, but it was the only interpretation that fit both the circumstances and the archetypical meanings of the cards in pattern.

She exposed the Five Swords above, and Judgment Reversed in front of him. Nine of Wands Reversed in the 9th, and in the tenth, World Reversed.

He fears failure, is beset on all sides, is pitied and hates it, knows he's beaten. Deep down inside, he wants to be caught, but is terrified of what will happen then.

All at once, she realized her mouth had been babbling words, and she clamped it shut as one final word exploded into her consciousness. *Suicide. If he fails, he plans to kill himself!*

She found herself gazing into hard, black eyes set in a face gone suddenly pale beneath a Florida tan.

What did I say aloud? She had no idea.

"Who!" he demanded. "Who's the police spy?"

Her throat emitted strangled noises.

His hand slapped the table, bouncing the cards. "Who!"

She forced her eyes back to the cards, expecting the images to be ten disconnected entities devoid of meaning. But the story was still clear. "A young woman you admire and trust, the one person you'd never suspect." *Oh, God! Why did I say that?*

He subsided into his chair, shocked wonder suffusing his face. "Of course! I should have known. All the clues were there and I couldn't see it." His attention snapped back to the cards. "What will happen if I just don't show?"

She swallowed and gritted her teeth, wishing desperately for Titus to walk in, then awash in relief that he wasn't there, she said, "I don't know. How could I possibly know? I can't foretell the future." Her voice broke into a squeak.

"Look at the cards. Tell me!" He was sweating. When she didn't move, he slapped the second three bills down on top of the first and reached into his breast pocket again to pull forth another three. He waved them at her as if she were an informant holding out for a higher bribe.

She wanted the money. She suddenly realized she'd been wrong all evening. The challenge wasn't to resist

Titus. The challenge was to resist abuse of power. Overwhelmed with shame, she recalled the ruddy glow of pride she'd felt when the crowd around her had murmured in awe. And there had been greed, too, as she saw the money being heaped into her bowl.

When she lowered her eyes again, the cards were just bits of colored paper. It would serve her right if she could never read again. She shook her head. "I don't know. Nobody can know. If I said something, it would be a lie." She pushed the money back across the table at him. "I was only guessing, and I was probably wrong." Relief sighed through her like a mountain breeze. Truth was its own reward.

He sat back and stared at her, stone faced.

She gave the money another little shove, and began collecting her cards.

On the periphery of her vision, she saw his hand move, flashing a heavy gold ring and watch. The next moment, hard hands gripped her wrists and she was yanked to her feet.

One of the men slammed the door of the room, while simultaneously, a hand clamped over her mouth and she was pinned against at tall, hard body. "She knows too much!"

"No. She's a charlatan like all the others. She was just guessing. It's not hard. Most everyone here knew we had a shipment coming in tonight."

"Well, if she didn't learn it from her cards, she certainly knows it all now. We have to make sure of her."

Gabby's heart slammed against her ribs. She could hardly breathe, but she prayed with all her might. *Are You really sure this is what You want? I'm sorry for what I did. I've learned a lesson. Isn't that enough? Do I have to die, too?* And aside, in her mind, the thought came, *Oh, Titus!*

If she hadn't tried so hard to read her own future in the cards before she came, she'd probably have gone with him instead of into the house, and none of this would have happened. *The cards can't foretell the future. Why can't I learn that?*

The man before her nodded to one of his men. "Take care of it." He went to peer out the little window which had a view of the steep slope behind the house. "Up there. See the rock? Drop her over the edge of that. Get some liquor into her first. Regrettable accident." He turned. "Anybody seen a phone on this floor?"

He went out and before she knew it, Gabby was wrapped around and tied securely by her sister's shawl. Somebody's silk handkerchief was tied around her mouth. That hurt. Her mouth was already dry, her voice husky with overuse. But she struggled anyway. She managed to kick the money bowl over as they dragged her out of the room. It made a satisfying crash. But nobody came. Nobody noticed as they carried her down the narrow, twisting back staircase, and past the dark and deserted kitchen. The fifth man, the one she'd been reading for, joined them and led the way out the back door.

Vines and branches slapped her face, cold dew

mixing with the hot tears that dripped from her eyes trailing backwards up her forehead because she was upside down.

She found herself being carried up the steep path she'd spotted from the front garden. Where it passed under the trees, the underbrush had been cut back forming a tunnel. A very dark tunnel. She struggled, hoping the man carrying her would trip and fall. Her moving weight did cause him to stagger. He slung her to the ground and slapped her face. "Stop it, or we'll all have at you before we dump you."

She glanced at the leader, who was carrying a large bottle of liquor. He seemed disinterested. Well, it would take up some time. Anything for a reprieve. It was a nice, logical thought but when the man shouldered her body once more, she couldn't bring herself to further defiance. *What's wrong with me? People survive rape!*

Before she could talk herself into it, she was rolled onto a cold, hard surface that was almost smooth. It sloped to one side and she rolled involuntarily, which brought the panorama of the Hudson River into view. There were fewer buildings lit now, and moonlight was coming from the west. But it was still breathtaking. *Oh, Titus!*

When she looked to see what her captors were doing, she found them passing the bottle. The last one wiped his mouth and let out a gusty sigh. "Too good to waste on her."

"Let's get this over with," said the leader as if he really didn't want to kill her. "Take the gag off and hold her mouth open."

One of them moved behind her and propped her up, cutting the gag and tilting her chin back. "Pour."

Another man held the neck of the bottle up to her mouth. "Drink. It'll make this easier on you."

Liquor gurgled into her mouth. She gathered it in her cheek, and when the man holding her clamped his fingers over her nose, she sprayed the stuff out hard. Even without swallowing it, the fumes triggered a coughing fit.

Someone slapped her face.

"Take it easy," said the leader. "We don't want to leave any evidence of a fight. I want this done perfectly."

The one holding her head shifted his grip and one hand crept down her back toward her buttocks. "Drink, girl, or you'll get it right in there!"

She yelped and surged away from his stiff finger, glad of the layers of thick skirt she wore.

Both hands came back to her head again. "Pour!"

Her head was forced back. She saw the five men in vampire costumes silhouetted against the stars as they bent over her. Higher up the sheer mountain, a very large oak leaned out above the rock. There was no wind, but the branches shook as she fastened her eyes on them and tried to pray. *I said do what You will with me. I meant it. Honest.*

Deep in the shadow, there was a figure hanging from the biggest branch. It looked human.

Without warning, the oak heaved and a blood curdling scream split the air. The man holding her jerked back, gasping, and the others turned. There above them, blotting out the sky, was a huge bat with red eyes and needle sharp teeth gleaming in the moonlight. Teeth and talons dripped thick, red blood. As it fell on them, engulfing them in a putrid stench, it screamed again.

She could feel the gust of wind from its powerfully beating wings. The sense of horror that washed through her made her previous terror seem like a silly illusion.

The man behind her dropped her. The liquor bottle fell and broke. The creature screamed again. In a mad scramble, the men ran. And something was settling down to eat her.

Without transition it seemed, Titus was bending over her, rubbing her wrists and patting her face. "Gabby? Gabby, are you all right? Wake up. Come on. You can do it. You only fainted. It's all right now."

She was untied and Titus's Dracula cape was laid over her like a blanket. "I must have passed out. You'll never believe what I thought I saw."

"What did you see?"

"It—" No, he'd never believe it. She didn't believe it. "Where did you come from?"

"The tree. I jumped down yelling, and those men ran."

She struggled to sit up. "Men. It wasn't a nightmare. It really happened. They were going to kill me. You were right. There were dealers here." That much was real, but the rest, the whole house had been thick with smoke. God alone knew what sort of drug mixture she

had in her blood by now. Small wonder she'd halluci-
nated.

"Can you walk, Gabby? We'd better get out of here.
They might come back."

She got up and took off his cape. It was too long. No
matter what she did with it, she'd trip on it. "Come on.
My car's out front," she said, trying to sound brave.
She doubted she even sounded sane. *Shock. It's shock.*
But even now, nothing seemed quite real.

He took her hand and led her down the dark, twisting
trail as if it were broad daylight.

There were still lights on in the house. "Titus, I'm
not going back for my things. Where's your car?"

"Don't worry about me. Just get yourself out of here."

They picked their way around the house as quietly as
they could, then dashed down the long flights of steps
to 9W. Panting, afraid they'd been heard, she paused,
one hand groping in her belt pouch for her car keys.
"Titus, how can I thank you for saving my life?"

"By not dying now. Are you sure you can drive?"

She held out the car key. It wasn't shaking. Yet.
"Sure. They didn't get any liquor into me. But what
about you?"

He walked her to the Mazda. "Don't worry about
me. Just get yourself away. I have my own transporta-
tion."

As she unlocked the door, he opened it and eased
her into the driver's seat. He leaned over and brushed
her forehead with his lips. "Go!" He closed the door
quietly.

Feeling beautiful again, she started the motor and eased away from the wall, catching sight of him in her right side mirror. The red lined cape was billowing in the wind like wings, and a stray bit of moonlight made his eyes glow red. She thought she saw a shimmering aura around him that throbbed with power. It had to be an optical illusion. It wasn't at all like any aura she'd ever seen before.

She shuddered.

Oh, come on! Don't be ridiculous. The combination of passive drug smoking with liquor fumes must have warped her brain.

"I jumped down yelling and those men ran." Fifty yards away and picking up speed, she glanced into her rear view mirror again, suddenly unable to understand why she had believed it when he'd said it.

Why had she scoffed at the thinness of his profile while forgetting that he'd lifted her up the steps quite easily? And what had he been doing in the tree? She was a reporter. She didn't fail to ask obvious questions like that.

She was also not stupid. She couldn't fail to see the obvious answer; *he is a real vampire.*

Her skin crawled and she clamped her chattering teeth together, determined to get home before she had any kind of reaction. At least she was headed south into New Jersey. She'd pick up Route 4 at the G.W. Bridge and be home in no time. Then she could shake and cry until dawn.

Vampires disintegrated at dawn and reality returned

full force. *That's what I need. A dose of reality.*

Titus was probably the police spy she'd thought was the Page of Swords. That was why he was able to handle those men so well. He was trained for this kind of thing, and he just wanted her out of there so the bust would go down smoothly. She'd see the whole thing on Eye Witness News in the morning.

And she'd never see him or anyone from that party again, including her boss. She'd call in her resignation in the morning, borrow some money from her mother, take off for California.

She clung to that resolution all the way home.

TRUE HOSPITALITY

"True Hospitality" is the direct sequel to "False Prophecy," which is a prequel to the novel *Those of My Blood* by Jacqueline Lichtenberg. info: http://www.simegen.com/jl/

At two thirty in the morning, there were no parking places on Gabby's street. She had to park around the corner and walk to the dilapidated three family house where she had the attic apartment. She tiptoed up the stairs, not wanting her tread to wake everyone.

She showered, rinsed out the dirty and torn witch's costume she'd worn to read Tarot at the Halloween party, and was still too overwrought to sleep. In nightgown and robe, she pulled out her suitcases and emptied her closet and drawers into them. Everything still fit. Since she'd moved out of her mother's house, she hadn't had the money to buy clothes.

While she packed, she made lists of things to do before leaving town. She'd have to store her dishes, tv, stereo, and microwave at her mother's. Everything else would fit in the car, which needed servicing. She could be in LA or maybe San Diego by the end of next week.

Even though her mind kept up a patter of orderly

planning, another part of her was gibbering, arguing, screaming to jump in the car, drive straight down to Newark and get on a plane using her credit card. Of course, organized crime could trace her through the card use.

She told herself the thought was paranoid. Why should they bother? So what if she'd read Tarot for a superstitious drug dealer who had tried to murder her at the Halloween party whereupon a vampire had rescued her.

Oh, come on! In the bright light of her apartment, she could believe she'd just been spooked out by the drug-smoke at the party and some realistic costumes. Titus had surely been an undercover cop in a really good Dracula costume.

But every time the old house creaked or a board popped, she could think of a thousand reasons why they might be coming after her. She schooled herself not to listen to the noises.

By the time she latched the last suitcase, her hands were shaking, her stomach was queasy, and her plans had crystallized. As soon as it was late enough, she'd drive straight to her mother's, borrow the money she'd need, and hit the road. Everything else could be handled by phone or mail, leaving as little trace as possible.

She had started packing the contents of her desk and a few light housekeeping essentials into boxes when there was a thumping in the hall.

There shouldn't be anyone on her landing this time of night. Heart in mouth, she froze in the middle of the living room, eyelids peeled back so far her eyeballs felt cold.

The door handle moved.

Like a horror movie.

She pulled her robe around her and crept toward the door. "Who is it?"

A man's voice grunted.

With her hand on the door handle, she felt the strength of the one who had hold of the other side of the handle. She grabbed the telephone that was close to the door. "I'm calling the police!"

"It's Titus!" the voice groaned. Titus' voice. "Gabby, please. Let me in!"

She dropped the half-dialed phone and scrabbled at the locks on the door, fumbled to get the inside key into the lock, and finally yanked the door open. Titus had been slumped against the door, and as she opened it, his body fell across the threshold. She leaped back with a squeal.

Whimpering, he mumbled, "May I please come in?" There was blood all over his face and hands but it was a mannerly request.

Instantly, she was on her knees beside him. "Dear God, what happened to you? Can you move? I don't think I can lift you inside."

His hand groped for purchase on her wrist. "Help me."

He tried to pull himself in, and she dragged him the rest of the way. With the door closed, cutting off the frigid draft, his shaking and moaning subsided. Shock.

Elevate the feet. Keep him warm. "I'll call an ambulance."

She grabbed for the phone, but he kicked it away. "No!"

"You need a doctor!"

His voice was stronger this time. "I'll be all right. Gabby they control the hospitals!"

Her imagination supplied the image of them. *Which means he's not with the police.*

The man had saved her life. She bent to examine the wounds. "Is anything broken? Have you been shot?"

"No, just scratches. I'll be—" He broke off with a gasp as she pulled at his blood stiffened jacket and new, bright blood flowed.

"You *have* been shot!"

"No. The business end of a garden rake."

As the stiff material came away in her hands, she saw it was in shreds.

"Just hide me until morning, and I'll be out of here," said Titus.

"It was the dealers, wasn't it? You went to spy on their business."

"Yes, I was there. The police got them." He twisted with a grimace and reached his right hand up to her face, one finger extended to touch her between the eyes. "*Most* of them."

Regardless of the risk, I have to call the police. It was her last truly coherent thought. His voice continued, a cascade of soothing sound that seemed to make compelling sense. She didn't understand why she was doing as he asked, but she never thought to question her motives.

She helped him up onto the sofa, which was vinyl covered, and wouldn't be ruined by the blood. Then, she stripped him and bathed his wounds with warm water, not bothering with disinfectant or soap, and gave him her robe to wear.

Titus rolled his head aside to eye one of the large bay windows, gray with approaching dawn. "What time is it?"

"Six thirty-five."

"A closet. Gabby, you must have an inside closet with no windows?

"The bedroom."

He struggled up. "That will do." His arm came heavily onto her shoulders. "Help me."

She supported him and guided him to the bedroom. "You think they'll shoot you through the windows?"

"No. I'm pretty sure no one could have followed me. I wouldn't put you in danger. Surely you know that."

She knew it beyond any doubt. "But what's an astrophysicist doing—you're not a dealer, too? A rival?"

They stopped in the bedroom door as Titus raked the display of suitcases, the empty closet and drawers with shocked eyes, but said, "No! Please believe me, Gabby. I wouldn't ever get mixed up in dealing."

The patent absurdity struck her like a douche of cold water. "But you are mixed up in it. Just look at you!" Suddenly, the world took on the bright, hard edges of normality. The sharp contrast was frightening.

Everything she'd just done for Titus seemed like some kind of bizarre charade, a mere pretence of help.

Once again, his voice lowered and hit some resonance that set her bones humming, leaving his words indistinct but his meaning perfectly clear. She answered what she thought he'd said with dramatic sincerity, "No, Titus, of course I won't tell anyone what you're about to tell me."

"Good. You see, I'm a real vampire. But I try very hard not to hurt people. I'm here to chase down a vampire who enjoys killing. He *is* mixed up in drugs. He was about to kill a woman who had infiltrated his organization, a police spy, so I tried to stop him. I got caught, but she got away. Then the police arrived and in the fight, my man escaped and so did I. You're going to protect me in your closet until sundown, and by then I'll be healed. We're safe here until then, so don't worry. After that, we'll go our separate ways, and you'll never see me again."

A large bubble of hysteria rose into her throat but could not erupt past the invisible choker that paralyzed her tongue. Delivered with a straight face, that story would easily have won the "Most Humorous" category in the Dracula contest.

At his behest, she brought him the two pillows off her bed and he made himself comfortable on the closet floor. As he closed the door, he flashed her an engaging grin. "Sundown."

She stared at the thickly layered paint on the old door. *I've got a vampire sleeping in my closet.*

She glanced at the window. Trees were etched against the brightening sky. It was 6:39 a.m. and she had a vampire sleeping in her closet. A very polite vampire who said please and thank you, hadn't sucked her blood and hadn't ravished her in her own bed.

She was suddenly possessed of a violent urge to yank the door open, certain there would be nothing there.

Her hand froze on the knob, and for all her will, all her years of discipline, she could not turn that knob.

In a pleasant, conversational tone, Titus said, "I won't be sleeping very deeply, Gabby. But I do need to rest. I know I can trust you."

Her bones ached. Her stomach churned. She let out a strangled sound that might have been agreement and plunged out of the bedroom. She ended up in the kitchen, leaning on the table, watching the red ball of fire rise into the sky. An astrophysicist was a little like an astronomer, and probably worked nights, too.

As the sun cleared the horizon of city buildings and haze, she remembered the purely physical feel of her hand on the closet doorknob, the locked resistance in her muscles, not the knob itself. No. Not in her muscles. In her mind.

She dragged in one sobbing gasp and slumped into a chair, burying her face in her hands. Her whole world conception turned inside out. Her breath exploded from her in a thin wail. "No. It can't be. Hypnotism. Illusion. Whatever. It's not what it seems." No real vampire would just calmly admit to it and settle down into a closet for the day. What about the "native earth" requirement?

But he had said he wouldn't sleep deeply.

Lips compressed, she shoved herself to her feet and went into the living room to retrieve the phone handset. She tiptoed into the bedroom, grabbed up the jeans and shirt she'd intended to drive in and eased the bedroom door shut.

She'd call her sister and confess she'd ruined the Halloween costume she'd borrowed. She always felt better after talking to Marlene.

Fully intending to tell her the whole story, she poked the number into the phone, triumph stretching her lips into a grin as she met no resistance. The phone rang once, twice, then a pleasant voice recited the time, date, and weather report, suggesting another number to call for air travel weather, domestic and international.

When the message began repeating, she held the handset at arm's length and stared at it. She knew no such service number. Had never dialed it before. And she knew she'd dialed her sister's number correctly. Surely they couldn't have jiggered her phone line to divert her calls?

She hung up, got a dial tone, and carefully re-entered the number. The same urbane synthesized voice came on again.

She hit the off button. She tried her mother's number and was connected to a religious message service.

She was only dialing a local number. She hadn't dialed enough digits to get toll service numbers.

Or had she?

When she put the phone down, the world seemed normal. But when she picked it up, her memory became hazy. She didn't notice it until she'd given up trying to tell people about Titus and put the phone away. Only after her mind cleared did she realize it had been clouded.

As she struggled into her clothes, she thought, *Maybe it's not the phone.*

She decided to call and cancel her gyn appointment since she would be gone by then. She looked up the number on the slip of paper tacked to the wall, and carefully poked it into the phone. The gyn's answering service came on, and using her phone buttons as instructed, she told their appointment computer to cancel her appointment. She hung up, called back, and checked to make sure her name was no longer on the schedule. *It's not the phone. It's me. Him, rather.*

Numb, she dropped onto the sofa.

The numbness wore off to leave stark terror, sharp edged and real, in its wake. The sun rose and the shadows of neighboring houses crept into the windows.

Finally, her mind began to work again. She made herself some coffee and toast, and spread out her Tarot cards to consider what to do.

Whatever he was, he had power over her. But, politely, he had used it in a very limited way. He had only protected himself. She was able to handle her personal affairs routinely. He had seen her packed bags and promised that she'd be free to go with the coming of sunset.

She believed him. Maybe that was his power. But if he hadn't meant it then why had he left her able to cancel her appointments? *If he's going to kill me, he'd want no one to be looking for me for a while.*

To test that, she decided to call her mother and ask for the loan she needed, make an appointment to pick up the check tonight. She entered the number. Her mother answered promptly.

"Mom. You were right."

"About what this time?"

"This is a dead end job. There's absolutely no future for me here. I've decided to go to LA, get a job, then reapply to UCLA. They accepted me before. No reason they wouldn't accept me again, especially as a California tax payer. But I need some money. If I leave tomorrow, I can be settled and establish residency in time to apply next year."

Since most of the plan had been her mother's idea originally, she had no trouble negotiating the loan, a check tonight and a more substantial sum when she had opened a bank account in California.

She solemnly promised to call her mother every day she was on the road, using her mother's phone credit card number.

Not one word stuck in her throat.

She called her sister and told the answering machine to look for the costume, in lamentable disrepair, at their mother's, and sketched her itinerary.

She called her boss, resigned with deep regret, telling him he had inspired her to go back to school. It was the literal truth. She didn't, however, give any hint of where she intended to go. She said she'd pick up her last check in the morning. The words didn't stick in her throat.

What I do tomorrow is no threat to Titus. He's not going to kill me.

She changed her mind and had her boss send her last check to her mother's post office box.

She called the bank and told the computer to close her savings account, dump all the money into her checking account and suspend all automatic payment of her bills.

She called a friend in LA and arranged herself a place to stay when she got there. She could sleep on the floor for a few nights. She even gave an estimated arrival time.

Everything she did regarding pulling out and arranging her future went without a hitch. The times she was tempted to say anything about a vampire, even in jest, her throat closed over the words in a way that made the reality of the unreal too believable.

When she'd done everything she could think of, she went back to the cards. The theme this time was the Tower, the Devil, the Chariot reversed, and the Magician reversed laced through with minor arcana indicating risk, combat, and anger. She'd seen worse readings about going to the dentist. But floating through the layouts, she kept noticing the Knight of Swords and the Knight of Wands.

Well, she was going to just up and leave, and that

would probably upset a lot of people. Staring at her notebook where she'd jotted down the three layouts, she wondered why nothing seemed to define Titus. And then she saw it.

Interpreting the layouts as Titus's readings, which was legitimate considering how she'd been concentrating on him as the problem, she knew with one of those clear, intuitive leaps that had begun coming to her at the party, that Titus's enemy, the killer vampire, had already traced Titus to her, had found out where she lived and would probably attack. Maybe tonight.

Her first impulse was to jump in the car and go. But again, the wordless compulsion seized her, leaving her glued to the kitchen chair. She had to protect Titus all day.

She stared at the cards. A reader couldn't really read for themselves without running grave risks, and she'd gone as far as she could go. She knew from experience that she'd get no more from the cards herself. She needed help.

She picked up the phone again to call her teacher.

Her hand froze on the phone as it had on the doorknob.

He's reading my mind!

The shriek of irrational panic subsided, and she realized it could just be the suggestion he'd implanted. After all, he'd said he didn't believe in the cards. *Imagine, a mind reading, hypnotizing vampire who rejects the psychic world!*

But if he didn't accept psychic abilities, he wouldn't

believe that Shawna would throw the cards a time or two and have the whole story before her. Gabby might not use the word vampire to Shawna, but she could describe the essence of Titus. Shawna was that good, and Gabby knew it, and so denied herself the help she most needed. *I can't make Shawna a target too.*

After another cup of coffee, she put the cards away in her handbag and returned to packing boxes. She had rented this place furnished, so there wasn't much that actually belonged to her. She labeled boxes for her mother to ship later, and some to take. She was pulling down the shower curtain when there was a knock at the door.

In a panic, she ran to the door and started to shove an empty book case in front of it. "Who—" Her voice squeaked. "Who is it?"

"Marlene. Who else at this hour?"

It was nearly three in the afternoon. With a sigh, Gabby shoved the bookcase back and opened the door. "What are you doing here?" She couldn't help it when her eyes darted to the bedroom.

Marlene swept into the room. She always entered a room with a sweep, and this time it was enhanced by the lush fake fur coat she flourished and dropped onto the vinyl sofa. But the theatrics were such second nature to Gabby's baby sister, that she didn't miss the panicked glance at the bedroom.

Pulling an envelope from her purse, Marlene waved it and sidled toward the closed bedroom door. "Mother asked me to bring you this check. This is such a lovely time of day in this apartment. You should keep the bedroom door open to let the sun in from that window." She shouldered the door open, leaning on it just right to un-stick it. But the glance inside was anything but casual.

Disappointment turned to grim disapproval as she saw the pile of luggage in the middle of the bed. "Mother told me about your harebrained scheme. What's the family going to do with you so far away? You could just as easily go back to Columbia."

"I hated Columbia, and they hated me. Look, let's not rehash old arguments. My mind's made up."

"Can't be. Yesterday, you were planning to help me make a New Year's party for the whole family, and today you're leaving tomorrow. That's not a decision, it's an impulse."

Sorely tempted to tell all, Gabby found her mouth stuck shut, and a rising urgency to get her sister away from the bedroom fought with an insane need to lie to protect Titus. She'd given up lying when she'd taken up the Tarot.

She took her sister's elbow and dragged her across the living room into the kitchen. "Come on, we can argue over coffee, and clean out the refrigerator."

Gabby dropped the check into her purse and spent the rest of the afternoon convincing her sister with lie after lie that just happened to be true. As they talked, they loaded most of boxes into Marlene's husband's Audi which she had just picked up from the shop.

There was a bundle of clothes on the way to the

cleaners in the trunk. That was supposed to go on top of the boxes because it had to be dropped off before Marlene went home. Gabby carried the laundry bundle upstairs and shoved it into a dark corner behind the rickety recliner that was missing a leg. Marlene's husband was about the same size as Titus.

Over the intervening hours, she genuinely forgot what she'd done and why.

Gabby never knew how she managed it, but she got Marlene to leave before full dark. Wiping tears of farewell from her cheeks, she went back into the apartment, locked the door, and leaned on it as her eyes watched the slice of sky visible above the bay window. A star appeared.

Switching on the overhead fixture, she saw the laundry bundle and panic seized her once more. *Why— how—did Marlene forget that! Why did I hide it away?* Her stomach churned. It had been hours since she'd thought of Titus.

A deep, male voice said, "My gratitude is as boundless as the cosmos."

"My God!" she squealed.

Titus, still wearing her bathrobe open over his tuxedo pants leaned over her, one hand propped on the wall by the door. He seemed pale, drawn, but the gashes in his side looked like year old scars, and the ones on his face and hands had disappeared. "Gabby, I'm sorry to have given you such a fright last night. You deserved better of me than that."

His hand floated out toward her face in an affectionate gesture. She jerked away. He froze.

"I won't hurt you."

"Get out." She was surprised she had the ability to voice the order. "Get out and don't ever come back. The invitation is withdrawn. Get out of here. I'll—I'll strew the place with garlic."

"Would you? Could you?"

Deep inside she knew she couldn't act against him. The imperative to protect him was stronger than she'd realized. "Maybe not, but I won't have to. Whoever did that to you last night," she gestured to the scars, "is going to be here soon."

He grabbed her shoulders so fast she couldn't react. Staring into her eyes, he demanded, "How do you know?"

The rest of the room blurred away, and all she saw were his eyes, all she felt were his hands on her shoulders, neither cold nor hot, just hands stronger than any she'd felt before. What spilled out of her was the absolute truth, though it's the last thing she'd have said willingly. "I saw it in the cards."

His breath gushed out of him in a warm cloud, not the stale stench of the Undead, just breath. Breath he had been holding with tension. He breathed regularly, not just when he needed to speak.

She slipped out of his loosening grasp and jackknifed over the recliner to fish out the bundle of laundry, turned and threw it at him. "Here! Take these and get out of here. Now! Because I'm leaving!"

She charged past him into the bedroom to collect her

suitcases. Turning back to the door with a case in each hand, she pulled up short. He stood blocking the door. Over one arm lay the shredded remains of his formal jacket.

"You told everyone you read for at the party that the cards can't predict the future."

"They can't. But everyone is psychic to some degree, we just can't access the knowledge of distant events in the present. Discerning them through the Tarot isn't predicting. It's not fate. You can be gone before he gets here. Then, too bad for him."

"I don't need Tarot cards to tell me I've got an enemy. And it doesn't take a fortune teller to divine that I need help." He advanced into the room, still blocking her way out of it.

She retreated. He stopped.

With his left forefinger, he rubbed the top of his forehead. "What I've already done to you is inexcusable—"

"I'll excuse it if you'll just leave."

"I can't."

There was real misery and genuine conflict in his eyes, his tone, his general aura. He was trying very hard to do something he believed to be right, but he wasn't sure he could manage. Gabby had no idea where that insight had come from, but she'd learned to trust her judgment about people. She edged to the side, trying to get a clear shot at the door. "Why can't you just leave?"

He looked at his feet as he whispered, "Hunger."

"Hunger?" *He's going to kill me.* Then she prayed,

Don't You think that's an awfully steep penalty for screwing up a temptation lesson?

"Hunger. I'm too weak to face him again, and I expect he'll find me before I reach safety tonight. I can't leave here in this condition, though I'm convinced we're safe here. At least for a while. Gabby, help me, please."

"That's a strange thing to say to someone you plan to kill."

"Kill?" He charged forward, tossing his jacket on the bed and brushed the suitcases out of her hands, grabbing her shoulders and pulling her to his chest all in one motion. "No! No, you don't understand. All I need is a little of your blood. Less than you'd give to the Red Cross. And I'll pay for it with the pleasure that is your due for such a precious gift."

She glanced aside at the open closet door, the pillows still visible on the floor. The edges were sharp. She checked her memory of what he'd said. It seemed clear enough. And now that he held her, the queasy feeling abated.

His arms were warm, strong but gentle. His lips brushing her forehead sent thrills coursing through her whole body. She buried her nose in his shoulder and just wanted.

The intensity of that unheralded desire was a shock. It was so different from anything she'd ever felt before that she hardly recognized it for what it was before it was too late. She pulled back, and was not quite surprised when he let her go. "What if I say no?"

"Would you do that, Gabby? I ask so little. I would

not leave you weakened. You'd be strong and ready for your trip."

"How do I know that?" But the cards had given no indication of real evil. And even now, the fog of perception he had used to force her to protect him was not in evidence.

"My word is not sufficient?"

"After the way you've forced me to help you, and prevented me from asking for the help I need—"

"Gabby, we have laws among our kind. If I had not silenced you, they'd hunt me down and kill me for endangering all of us. I had no choice in what I did to you. I've only a little choice now. Refuse me, and I will leave and take my chances."

"You mean, find someone else?"

"There's one thing I've discovered recently. I much prefer volunteers."

It was the slickest manipulative pitch she'd ever heard.

He moved in close again and stroked her cheek before she could shrink back. Sensation suffused her whole being and she groaned deep in her throat. His finger outlined her lips and she couldn't help tilting her head up to him. His touch trailed down her neck to her open collared shirt, then hesitated, asking permission.

Despite herself, she leaned into the touch, giving permission. She couldn't have denied herself at that moment to save her life. She no longer cared if she died, she had to have what he promised.

His perfectly groomed fingernail slid over the outside

of her bra, toyed with her nipple until her whole breast ached and then welcomed his hand as it worshiped the weight of it. "You see," he murmured into her ear, "there is much I have to offer in reward. And I ask so little."

She wanted to claw at him, climb onto him, force him not to stop now.

He pushed away, holding her at arm's length, his eyes meeting hers. "I am so hungry."

It was artless, the conflicts tearing at him so near the surface that she could see them. She pushed her own desire down and asked, "What do you want to do, bite my neck?"

He grimaced, his sensuous mouth making a straight line as he shook his head, loosed her arms, and picked up his jacket. The inside pocket yielded a Ziplock bag with a tourniquet and some sealed packages of disposable needles, the kind used to collect blood donations. He held the bag for her to see. "Nothing so dramatic. A couple of glassfuls will suffice."

She stared at the prosaic tools and for the first time really believed she was dealing with a true vampire, not legend, myth, maniac, or disease victim, but the real thing, the fact behind the fiction. And the world remained clear around her. That, more than anything, convinced her.

She had felt his power to coerce, and a moment ago had been thoroughly seduced by an equally powerful force. Yet still he held back, asking.

"Well, all right, just this once." she answered his

silence. "But never again."

"If that's the way you want it to be, then that's the way it will be."

"What do I have to do?"

He took her into the kitchen where she sat at the table with her arm out while he tied the tourniquet, thumped the vein like a professional, swabbed the skin and inserted the needle. She had to look away as her blood, deep red, dripped into a jelly glass. Her arm was cold. Her back hurt.

His hand spread over the ache in her back and rubbed, making a delicious warm spot. "Not much longer now," he crooned, and she could hear the barely restrained greed in him. "There!" The needle was gone with a cold sting of alcohol, and the tourniquet released with an audible snap. He was gone before she turned her head back.

Her arm was crooked up around the alcohol swab. The needle had been deposited in the trash. "They'll think I'm an addict!" she muttered without real panic.

She bared her elbow to look at the wound. *What have I done? Fed a vampire?* But he wasn't the legendary kind, the kind supposed to be Evil and Undead. He was just a man with strange needs and even stranger powers.

If she had cold-shouldered Titus outside the Halloween party house, he wouldn't have been there to save her life. If she hadn't gone to the party, she wouldn't have needed her life saved, but she would probably have lost her job. Yet, that's just where she was now anyway, jobless.

There was no sound from the living room. Thinking he might have just left, she got up and went to the door. The bathroom door was closed, and water was running. She hadn't actually seen him drink. He could have flushed it all down the toilet. The whole thing might have been some sort of charade.

Then she remembered how she'd tried to clean the stage makeup off of his face last night. That pasty whiteness was his natural complexion. And he was no albino. In fact, the albinos she knew had a lovely translucence to their skin. Titus looked like he was wearing zinc oxide coating all over his body.

She was about to turn back into the kitchen hoping he'd just leave now when the bathroom door opened. He had stripped and re-donned her robe, and as he moved toward her there was no doubt in her mind that he had drunk the blood and it had restored him to vitality as it would only to a vampire.

She couldn't say what it was about him, exactly, but he appeared more robust, calmer, stronger. He glided toward her now, and only by contrast could she see that before, his gait had been hesitant, shuffling, as if he were in pain. Now, he exuded controlled power.

His arms came around her and before she knew what had happened, she was in his arms, cradled against his chest as if she weighed no more than ninety pounds. "Did you think I'd forgotten my promise?" he breathed as he tilted her through the narrow bedroom door and gently set her on the bed.

His mouth covered hers, eager and willing, yet hesitant, asking permission. His whole attention seemed to be on her, seeking to learn what she wanted. Never had a man approached her this way before. All at once, the aching returned to her breasts.

From there a warm flush spread to everything else he touched. There was no mistaking his own intense arousal, but it seemed merely a reflection of her own, escalating at every thrilling stroke of his sensuous fingers. With tentative, dancing touches, those lithe fingers opened her clothing and began peeling it away, an inch at a time.

When he unhooked her bra, she gasped and he stopped. Then, slowly, he leaned down and kissed her again, silently stating his case. Deep inside, she knew this was her last chance to say no. She didn't want to, but she knew it would be prudent.

He shifted his weight until the physical evidence of her effect on him throbbed against her thigh. His right hand came to rest on her groin, perfectly still as if he'd forgotten what he touched as his whole attention focused on her lips and tongue.

She had never been so aroused in her whole life. She was dimly aware she was being seduced, but the experience seemed more important than any other consideration. After all, he wasn't forcing her. The edges of the world were still clear. It was her own decision, and she wasn't going to deny herself something this special.

She put her arms around his neck and kissed him back. His right hand began to move, and she realized that until that moment, she hadn't even begun to be aroused.

It went on for a very long time, longer than any man had ever spent on her before. Never once did she feel she had to hurry or miss out completely. It was almost as if he enjoyed simply being aroused as much as she did.

As the tension mounted and mounted, she began to wonder if he was incapable in some fashion. She worked one hand down between them and began to repay the intimate caresses.

He gasped, paused, and melted into her touch with a groan. She had him in total surrender. If that was what she wanted. She could pick the position and the time. No man had ever let her do that before. Still, his knowledge and skill outstripped her own by so much, she'd always wonder what she'd missed. "Go on," she whispered. "Do it. Your way."

Panting, he encircled her hand with his own and gently removed himself from her grip. "Not yet, Gavriella. You're capable of so much more." His hands and lips began another detailed study of her whole body, front and back, and ended with her feet, where attention centered and deepened.

Just when she thought she couldn't stand it any more, he moved up to lie beside her, then eased over her and entered without any help. Pure orchestrated sensation rose in every shred of her being. His lips covered hers once more, and gently, carefully, he teased her to the absolute apex, a condition she could never have imagined in her wildest dreams, a state no romance writer had ever evoked for her with the purplest prose.

Then it happened to both of them, simultaneously. But, in that ineffable, unspeakable moment, she felt his seed flood out from him onto her thigh.

The golden glory was tarnished, but still the greatest experience of her life. It became even greater when he didn't simply roll aside and begin to snore. He stayed with her, petting and stroking, thanking her body, appreciating it as much now as when he'd wanted something from her.

This must be what it's like to be loved.

By the light of the street lamps, she could see the same wonder reflected in his eyes.

When he eased himself to her side, and propped himself on one elbow to toy with her hair, she breathed, "Why! Why didn't you finish it right?"

He kissed her. "Neither of us could afford any unwanted complications. I didn't think you were protected."

"I'm not." She had taken that into account when she'd acquiesced, but at the time it had seemed a reasonable risk. Actually, she realized, it wasn't. "Still...."

Suddenly, his arms were around her again, and he whispered into her ear, "Gabby, I can't tell you what you've given me. You've opened up a whole new world of possibilities to me. I promise, when this is all over, I'll look you up again, and if it's what you want then, you will have it just the way you want it."

"You won't be able to find me," she mumbled, her

whole body and mind unraveling into deep relaxation.

"Don't worry about that."

He stroked her back, and she tumbled into sleep feeling more safe and protected than she had ever felt before. The entire experience had redefined what sex was about for her, and now she wasn't sure that was a good thing. Would any man ever measure up again?

Some undefined time later, she woke, aware she'd been asleep only by the fact that she was waking. She was alone in bed, the pillows restored for her comfort. It was still pitch dark outside, but she'd packed her alarm clock so she had no idea what time it was.

No light came through the crack under the living room door, but she heard Titus moving about. She didn't want him to leave like that, so she got up, found her robe neatly folded at the foot of the bed with her clothes. She flung the robe on and tucked the bundle of clothes into the crook of her arm, intending to shower and dress, then leave. She should have gotten them both out of there at sundown.

In the living room, by the streetlight, she found Titus just cinching up the waist of the borrowed brown pants using a strip torn from the black cummerbund he'd been wearing. Everything hung on him like a sack, but at least he was decent.

She crossed to him. "I wanted to say thank you."

"Oh, no, it is I who should—" He broke off, whirling toward the door in a crouch. "Gabby, get dressed!"

"What—"

"Do it!" He flitted across the floor and plastered

himself to the wall beside the door, one ear pressed to it as if listening. The street light picked out planes and shadows on his lean features.

Heart pounding, she skinned into her underwear and pulled her clothes on, shoving her feet into a pair of running shoes she'd left under the sofa.

Titus nodded. "It's him. Get your coat. I have to get you out of here."

He pulled open the closet door beside the bathroom, but that was the linen closet. She grabbed a fleece lined jacket from the shelf under the table where she kept her purse, slung her purse over her head and slid one arm through the strap. "Who is it, the killer vampire?"

"No. My father. Let's go!"

She started for the door, but he took her arm and swung her around. "No! This way."

He had the living room window open and was outside, standing on the roof of the porch with his hand out to her before she knew how he'd done it. She'd often contemplated using the roof as a fire escape, but it was almost a two story drop to the ground from the bottom of the slanted roof.

She closed her jacket over her purse, which contained everything of real value, including her mother's check. She'd long ago concluded that she was going to be running for her life, and somehow, she trusted Titus, even if he did have a facetious streak. *His father! Really!*

With one hand gripping her wrist and the other her elbow, he somehow levered her out of the window.

Then he paused to close the window and plastered himself against the side of the building pulling Gabby up beside him.

She held her breath as a shadow flitted through a distant, neighboring yard. It was a very tall, reed slender figure. It disappeared between two houses, heading for the back yards.

Meanwhile, a car purred to a stop at the end of the block and double parked. Four men got out, shutting the doors very quietly. Gabby clutched at Titus's arm as the men started toward them.

Titus breathed into her ear, "Where's your car?"

"Up around that corner they're blocking. About half a block up that street."

He sighed. "The car I used ran out of gas up on Four."

The idea of a vampire discommoded by running out of gas almost made her laugh.

"We'll have to take their car, then," he said.

The four men approached, scanning the bushes in every direction but never looking up. They moved up the steps very quietly, and opened the door as quickly as if they'd had a key. No sooner was the last one inside than Titus turned and swung Gabby up in his arms. Before she knew what was happening, he took two strides and stepped out into thin air.

If she'd had any warning at all, she'd have screamed on the way down. But before she could draw breath, Titus's feet touched the ground and his knees bent, absorbing the impact. By the time her buttocks touched the cold pavement, it was only a minor thump, less than if she'd fallen on the stairs.

"Shit!" she said. "How did you—"

His hand clamped onto her mouth. "Shh!" He bent to her ear. "Simple physics." His other arm gave her a confident squeeze, and then he was helping her to her feet. Pulling her behind him, he began to make his way through the yards, keeping bushes and trees between them and the double parked car. A feeling of unreality englobed her, and she could almost believe she was acting in a movie.

A distant part of her mind noted that the car they were about to steal from the drug dealers was a TransAm. They'd never have had a chance in her Mazda if the TransAm chased them.

Steal from the drug dealers. Steal a car from the drug dealers.

Something kept the natural panic that thought engendered at a great distance. She was glad for the distance. Panic could be fatal right now.

As they came abreast of the car, she could see the man left inside to guard it.

On a sudden thought, she dragged Titus back into the bushes and put her mouth to his ear. "What if those four men come back!"

"Don't worry. My father will take care of them. Now, let me concentrate."

Father. He meant it! "Why are we running from your father?"

"You don't want to know. Now, hush!"

In a few moments, the driver of the car lazily opened

the door and eased himself out. He left the door open and wandered haphazardly up the street. They waited until he was nearly half a block away, then dashed for the car.

Titus took the wheel, motioning her around to the other door. As she closed her door, Titus spun the car around in a tight U turn, slid into the right turn at the corner and gunned the motor as he guided the car down the middle of the street.

"How did you know that man would leave the key in the car?" she asked when they made it onto the Garden State without any sign of pursuit.

"Influence."

"What?"

"I used Influence, the power of my kind that so distresses you. I'm sorry, but there was no other way to avoid killing him."

Killing him. Titus had said the words as if he had every reason to believe it would have been just as easy to kill a man who was, very likely, a professional killer.

If this vampire worked that hard to avoid killing a murderer, she knew she was completely safe. "Where are we going?"

He grinned. "How about Los Angeles?"

"Sounds good. But all my things are in my car."

"Don't worry. You've earned a whole set of new things."

ABOUT THE AUTHOR

JACQUELINE LICHTENBERG is a life member of Science Fiction Writers of America. She is the creator of the Sime~Gen Universe with a vibrant fan following (www.simegen.com), primary author of the Bantam paperback, *Star Trek Lives!* (which blew the lid on Star Trek fandom), founder of the Star Trek Welcommittee, creator of the genre term Intimate Adventure, winner of the Galaxy Award for Spirituality in Science Fiction with her second novel, *Unto Zeor, Forever*, and the first Romantic Times Awards for Best Science Fiction Novel with her later book, *Dushau*, now in Kindle. Her fiction has been in audio-dramatization on XM Satellite Radio. She has been the SF/F reviewer for a professional magazine since 1993. She teaches science fiction and fantasy writing online while turning to her first love, screenwriting, focused on selling to the feature film market. She can be found at her website,

www.jacquelinelichtenberg.com

And can be followed on...

twitter.com/jlichtenberg
facebook.com/jacqueline.lichtenberg
friendfeed.com as jlichtenberg

www.ingramcontent.com/pod-product-compliance
Lightning Source LLC
Chambersburg PA
CBHW031401250626
47155CB00004B/1364